Everything's Basically Fine

by Daniel Bevis

Chapter One

The sound of a battered Ford Focus scraping along steel crash barriers isn't one I'd previously given a lot of consideration to, in the spectrum of interesting and noteworthy noises, but it's really quite insistent. I guess the fact that it's underpinned by an obvious and absurd layer of stupidity helps to elevate it to a howling and memorable crescendo. Maybe that's what's flagging it up as a noise worthy of further pondering. Or maybe it's the gunfire. Whichever way, it's the sort of absurd concatenation of circumstances that'd probably keep normal people up at night afterwards. But not me, I like to let things go. Well, sort of. That's what I tell myself, anyway.

It's a pretty unusual situation though, I have to say. I mean, compared to the average commute. I suppose terrorists, if that's what they are, I imagine they must be, are as partial to fashions and trends as anybody else; recent years have seen all sorts of mad bastards ploughing down pedestrians on bridges, pavements and shopping concourses the world over, just copying each other really, it's not an original idea, and they seem to particularly like bridges in London, although why they think it's a good idea to do it on Waterloo Bridge today is entirely beyond me. Waterloo Bridge has sturdy crash barriers along pretty much its entire length, separating pavement from road with a certain steely finality; you'd need some sort of armoured truck to spang through that with any level of murderous effectiveness. Trying to do it in an ageing hatchback is, quite frankly, moronic. They're embarrassing themselves.

It's usually a pleasant stroll, very Londony as commutes go – you've got the stark concrete brutality of the National Theatre and the Hayward Gallery ahead of you, the towering majesty of the Eye to the right, Big Ben just across the water, balefully encased in scaffolding right now but still presumably in there, I should think, and colourfully scudding pleasure boats below. Sure, it can be pretty grim when it's raining, but on a day like today, when there's barely a cloud in the sky and the sun's beaming like an old Vitalite commercial, you shimmer across the Thames with a bounce in your step and a song in your heart. Unless, that is, there's a car crunching past you in a shower of sparks, sprinkling little cubes of glass about the place as its occupants hysterically realise that their progress may be insurmountably impeded by a sturdy barrier which, now I come to think of it, is very well designed indeed. Look at it, doing its job with casual aplomb, shrugging off the onslaught of a tonne-and-a-half of speeding metal. Whoever bolted that together can luxuriate in the warming glow of a job well done.

Inevitably, of course, the car comes to a halt, haemorrhaging fluids and artfully mangled, while the scattered pedestrians who had been screaming and trying to run in four directions at once start to shift into another state, one of confusion and anger that someone's just tried to squash them and then failed quite publicly and stupidly. They swarm toward the wreckage, rightly vexed, and are caught totally by surprise by the gunman who leaps out of the car and starts spraying bullets into the crowd. At that range, and with that sort of weapon – and I know nothing about guns, but it's clearly something capable of pumping out rounds at a rate of knots – the number of casualties is bound to be dramatic. As bodies fall left and right, this proves to be the case. The mowing-everyone-down idea hadn't played out, but the backup plan is devastatingly effective.

I'm still marvelling at the effectiveness of the crash barrier, so it makes perfect sense to continue to enjoy its protective merits. I lie down on my side, tuck my knees into my chest, and simply hide behind the lower section of the metal fence. It works a treat. If life has taught me one thing time and time again, it's that curling yourself into a ball and pretending things aren't happening is a thoroughly effective technique, and if any bullets come my way, and I can't say for certain whether they have, they're skilfully deflected by that excellent sheet of steel. I can't see what's happening as my eyes are obscured by my knees, but the gunfire lasts for perhaps twenty or thirty seconds before the roar of the enraged mob overpowers it. When I peep up to assess how things are progressing, I see the gunman fly over me with dulled eyes, following a graceful arc above the pavement and down into the murky waters below. There appears to be a general sense of satisfaction at this state of affairs, although there are rather a lot of bodies strewn about the place, some vocal and some less so, which rapidly divert everybody's attention, and I suppose this is only to be expected.

There is a numbness, a hesitance. But as much by reflex as compassion, I dial 999 and give them a précis of events, suggesting that a large number of ambulances might be in order, then set about applying tourniquets and makeshift bandages to the ones who aren't corpses, patting their hands and trying to reassure them that the worst bit is probably over, and that it isn't all bad because it is nearly the weekend and Channel 4 are running a James Bond marathon, and look around you, things could have ended worse. It's hard to reassure people who've just been shot that they've somehow got off lightly, but it's really the only card I have to play at this point.

The emergency services' response times are famously good in London, particularly so in this instance it seems, and in merely a few blinks of an eye the bridge is abuzz with flashing lights and piercing sirens, as smartly uniformed paramedics swiftly identify which people to load onto stretchers, and equally polished policemen stride through the chaotic scene pinpointing the most useful-looking witnesses. I'm approached by a tallish chap with a stern manner, who has aggressive coffee breath but that's fine, we all need a pick-me-up at this time of day, and he writes down my contact details in his notebook. He has a nice pen, and I idly wonder whether policemen get issued with nice pens as a rule, or if he's drafted in his own fancy Parker with a marbled-effect finish in place of the regulation-issue Bic. I realise that he's been talking to me while I was wondering about pens and I haven't been listening.

"I'm sorry?"

"I asked you why you're smiling," he deadpans, his expression one of perfect blankness.

I can't think of an answer to this, as I've never really been much of a smiling person, but he seems busy enough so when he's distracted by a colleague I simply walk away in the direction of the train station. The authorities appear to have this under control now, and if I walk briskly and take the overground route, because the underpass past the IMAX isn't the short-cut it appears to be, although I do enjoy the busker who's been playing the accordion down there this week, I might still make the 17:47.

I'd be interested to know what it's like to believe in something so passionately that you're willing to kill for it. I imagine it requires some pretty deep reserves of anger and resentment. Something better suited to the old me, I used to be angry, I used to get worked up by the littlest things, raging at coffee shop workers who'd cocked up my order, swearing at petrol pumps for clicking over to £20.03 when I only had a twenty on me, beating my dad's face to a mushy caricature when he left my mum and abandoned us both when I was supposed to be concentrating on my GCSEs, wishing mechanical death upon the dishwasher when it always left that horrible filmy sediment at the bottom of the beer glasses. But I've let it all go. Last year I decided that none of it mattered. I mean, in the grand scheme of things, what does? Yes, you can be angry about life, but the outcome will be largely the same whether you are or not, so why not just let it all wash over you? It's probably healthier in the long run.

This new way of living has freed me from complexity. It's like floating on the pillowy effects of some wonderful drug. I see people all around me stressing about their phone reception and their insurance renewals and their communicable diseases, and it all just seems so ridiculous. I am calm. I am mellow. Everything's basically alright, isn't it? And given a long enough timescale, it all reduces down to nothing anyway.

———————————————————

The man behind the counter in the corner shop is eyeing me suspiciously, and it takes a few moments to process the likelihood that it's all the blood on my clothes that's making him jittery. I expect people who've just committed the sort of violent attacks that lead to their clothes being saturated with blood tend to conduct themselves in an aggressive and edgy manner, so I make a special effort to exude cooling waves of calmness and serenity, in order to reassure him that I'm on the helpful side of tragedy rather than the chaotic one. Besides, for all he knows I could be an artist who works in the medium of stickily coagulating crimson oil paints. Or a ham-fisted butcher who hasn't got the hang of filleting yet. What he sees and what he knows are two very different things.

My purchases surely reassure him that I'm not a nutter; chicken breast, red onion, garlic, vegetable stock, basmati rice, nigella seeds, butterscotch Angel Delight, non-specific reasonably priced red wine of provenance unknown. This is not the shopping of a lunatic. Is it? I could explain what had just happened on the bridge, but I imagine there would be follow-up questions and ideally I'd like to get home sharpish and get the dinner on before *Goldfinger* starts. And anyway, I come in here quite a lot, and we've only just normalised our balanced customer-shopkeeper dynamic after the, er, scratchcard incident last June, when I thought I'd won a sizeable prize and he patiently pointed out that I'd misunderstood the game and had actually won a pound, and there may have been a bit of a scene, but it wasn't his fault, I was cross, but I wasn't sure who with, and he was nearest, I think I might have called him some things, but it feels like time might have healed some of this so really there's nothing to worry about is there?

We're OK here. The transaction is completed in a friendly enough manner and I even offer him a 'cheery-bye' as I leave, which I've never said before but it seems to be the sort of thing that breezy and carefree people say, and he doesn't act affronted by it so I think we can take that as a win.

There's a glorious crispness in the air as I stroll down the high street, observing the trees energetically sprouting their buds and unfurling their perfect little leaves. Even the eddying swirls of crisp packets and discarded nightclub flyers have a certain majesty to them as they dance in their miniature tornados, the lark's on the wing and the snail's on the thorn and so on, but my hands are starting to shake and there's an iciness tickling at my soul, so it seems prudent to nip into the coffee shop for a warming infusion of something highly caffeinated, just to take the edge off. The walk home from here is only ten minutes or so, and that little endorphin spike will carry me back a treat.

The barista has the same look in his eyes as the man in the corner shop did, but that's fine, I don't think there's any judgement, and does it really matter if there is, our relationship is pretty straightforward here, he makes drinks out of beans and I give him money for it, no need to overcomplicate anything. I can feel that he understands this. I idly wait for a couple of minutes for my flat white to be prepared, flicking through the leaflets on the counter detailing muffin recipes and primary school jumble sales, and then I'm handed a cup which is clearly too large to house a standard flat white, but there's no-one else here and the cup has my name scrawled on it, kind of, give or take a few vowels, so it's clearly what I ordered. Must be.

A few hundred yards down the road, it turns out to be a vanilla latte. That's kind of annoying. Should I go back and complain?

No, no point. Vanilla lattes are fine, aren't they? I think vanilla is much misunderstood, actually. It gets a really hard time, people say it's a boring flavour choice. The brainless default, the drab, beige option you only opt for if you can't be arsed to think about it, or if there's nothing else available. Out of rum 'n' raisin? Yeah, I guess I'll have vanilla. You bought the new Ed Sheeran album? Oh, that's so vanilla. Your fondness for missionary intercourse is just vanilla. *Vanilla vanilla vanilla*. It's not fair, it really isn't, vanilla used to be such a revered and exciting little bean, I believe it's derived from orchids, and there aren't any more precious or delicate flowers than those, and I seem to remember reading that its cultivation dates back to the Aztecs, and every single vanilla pod has to be pollinated by hand, and it's a lot more special than anyone gives it credit for, even if most mainstream vanilla flavouring these days is synthetic, vanilla as a concept is actually very special and we should really try to appreciate that fact a little more.

All that being said, if I'd wanted a fucking vanilla latte I'd have fucking ordered one, *for fuck's sake*. But that's by the by, I suppose. It tastes fine, it's not worth stressing about. Don't lose it. Stay calm.

The house is cold, which suggests that the creeping optimism of spring still hasn't quite found its feet in the bits of the world that don't smell richly of chlorophyll. Do I flick the heating on? Why not, have a treat, it's been an unusual day.

After a cursory piddle I set about slicing the red onion into slender half-moons, and shaving the garlic with a razor blade because that's what they do in *Goodfellas* and it feels like an artisan way to go about it. Then I heat the pan, splash in a little olive oil, break down in a heap on the kitchen floor and bawl my eyes out for three or four minutes, then throw the garlic and onions into the pan to sizzle while I snip up the chicken with scissors. I don't see the point of cutting it with a knife on a chopping board, that just makes two things to wash up instead of one.

After I put the rice on, and before I pour myself a generous glass of the cheap red, I treat myself to another session of desperate sobbing, straight from the diaphragm, really deep. The blood on my clothes and skin is starting to smell distinctly like old pennies. I feel like I should leave it on me for a while, just a little while longer, in order to collect my thoughts and absorb what happened.

Not that it requires deep analysis, of course. I was there, the thing happened, I did what I did, and now I'm here. What happens out there rarely affects the bit of evening when you're sitting on the sofa with telly and wine and mum on the mantelpiece as the anxiety simmers gradually away, does it? It's the happy place, the secluded cell that blocks out the outside world.

Cell. Is that a positive word? Not really.

The telephone rings in the happy place. It's Detective Chief Inspector Wilson, who wants to come round and ask me some questions tomorrow evening. I tell him that this is completely fine.

Chapter Two

There's a sparkling freshness to the world this morning, artfully reframing the gloomy mist as a haze of hope rather than the expected pessimism. Yes, it's grey and soupy, but it feels like it'll all burn off soon, and that could possibly be some sort of metaphor for a brighter future that I'll have to have a little think about as I amble to the station.

The schoolchildren coming in the opposite direction are derailing this train of thought somewhat, although if they want to ride their bikes on the pavement I suppose that's their prerogative. There was a time when I would have phoned the school to complain about their flagrant disregard of the law regarding bicycles and pavements, I mean, I'm pretty sure that's a law, right, seems like the kind of thing that would be, and their unwillingness to wear helmets, and the manner in which they careen on the very fringes of control as they pull endless wheelies while darting in and out of pedestrians' paths, but this kind of bellyaching is fruitless. And besides, they're just kids. Kids can be excused, they're not thinking about the long game, they haven't learnt the nuances of grown-up social interaction yet. When the boy in the presumably inadvertent Hitler Youth haircut crashes square-on into me and takes all the wind from my lungs, I just grimace a little and let him pass. Because what's to be gained from berating him?

The necessity of sitting on a low wall and gathering my breath for a few minutes means that I arrive at Stoneleigh station with a mere thirty seconds to spare before the train is due to arrive, although – with a certain reassuring inevitability – the train is cancelled and the following one is running fourteen minutes late, which is all just part of the colourful and laissez-faire approach to timetabling that makes this rail operator such an engaging company to deal with. Every day is a fresh surprise. You get plenty of time to sit and read at the station while waiting for a train which may or may not arrive, so it's as if the rail company is giving you the gift of time itself. There is no present more generous.

As one might expect, the cancellation of a rush-hour train means that the next one is rather busier, and I find myself sandwiching into a game of human sardines, a vibrantly fruity armpit masking my face from reality with its zesty tones of third-day-of-a-music-festival robustness. After ten minutes of being roundly jostled and elbowed in soft places, the guard announces over the tannoy that the train will now be running fast to Waterloo, so anyone who needs intervening stations has to get off and wait for the next one. Before the recent office move, this would have been me, and on a day like to today, what's the hardship, the sun is burning off the mist just as I suspected, it's beginning to look rather lovely, but now that Waterloo is my destination I'm free to squish into a corner as a stream of apoplectically enraged commuters disembark to send some very cross tweets. I consider suggesting the merits of letting go of one's anger, but conclude that starting the day with a punch in the face is probably counter-productive. Having survived being run over and shot yesterday – well, cunningly hidden behind a barrier, anyway – it would be most unfortunate to be hospitalised the following morning by a grumpy loss adjuster with a rolled-up Metro and a damaged approach to losing twenty minutes of his day to signalling issues. As with so many situations in life, the method here is to simply melt into the background and let the world wash around you. I find myself doing this a lot these days.

Waterloo is bristling with armed police, as you might imagine. Officers who presumably haven't seen that *Bourne* film, whichever one it is that has the Waterloo scene, because they're solely eyeballing the throngs on the concourse rather than looking upwards to where the better hiding places are. But in spite of the chaos I'm keen to retain a sense of normality – because why wouldn't you? – so, M&S croissant and Boots meal deal acquired, I stroll out of the front entrance. They had the nice smoothies in stock today, the mango ones with the coconut milk, so things are really looking up. Sometimes fate does smile on you. It's great when things work in your favour, isn't it? This might be a good day.

The accordion player in the underpass is as jolly and cherry-cheeked as ever, and I stop to listen for a couple of minutes before rooting in my pockets for a coin, realising that I spent my last pound coin on the croissant, giving him a reassuring 'maybe tomorrow' grin and making my way along the tunnel. I'm not sure where he's from or what language he speaks, so presumably the words he mouthed at me weren't actually 'fucking cheapskate', but what if they were? I'll walk the overground route tomorrow, and he'll forget I exist, and the cosmos will slide back into its natural equilibrium as ever it shall. It's at once the worst and best constant of reality, that nothing ever lasts.

The bridge, perhaps unsurprisingly, is cordoned off. I say 'unsurprisingly', but it surprised me, I should've considered the possibility of that, as now I'll have to take a hefty detour to cross a different bridge and will be even later for work, but no, that's fine, the extra exercise certainly won't do me any harm, and the variety will be welcome. London's nice to look at, I'm OK with looking at some different bits.

I stand for a moment to take in the scene behind the cordon, albeit from a necessary distance demanded by the copious officers present. Around the spot where I'd found my haven by the barrier there's a sizeable patch of blood, dark and rich and sticky like tar, and the pavement is littered with little numbered flags on poles indicating every shell casing, every spilled splash of claret. I find myself unable to stop staring, but an encouragement to *'move along sir, move along, sir, go, go now'* urges me down onto the South Bank.

I'm walking slowly and distractedly, not picking up my feet, scuffing the soles in a way that would once have elicited maternal chastisement. A teenager with a skateboard calls me a wanker, for some reason, and his mates snigger, but that's alright, we were all young once.

The atmosphere in the office is crackling with excitement, in the manner it was the day after the 7/7 bombings, and Grenfell, and all the other colossally horrible things that happen to this city all too regularly, the genuine sadness and mourning of the few muddles colourfully with the pseudo-grief and actual excitement of the many, and nothing's getting done because everyone's picking over the details. I don't blame them for being excited. A terror attack within walking distance of the office? Ooh, it's so *juicy*. I entertain the possibility of making it known that I saw the thing happen, but these people have made it abundantly clear to me that they don't want me here or have any interest in any of the things I have to say and I don't wish to annoy them – far be it from me to dilute their giddiness over so many thrilling deaths, I'll just take my croissant to my desk and let them get on with comparing body counts like Top Trumps, they're happy in their vulture-like gloating, that's cool.

Inevitably my chair has been swapped for somebody else's and my keyboard and mouse have been unplugged and my mug liberated, so I go through the morning routine of reassembling my workstation while images of the flying gunman flash through my head. That's healthy isn't it, to be picturing him? I'm sure it'll help with police identification if nothing else. The shooter looked quite a lot like Jed, the senior manager who insisted upon my disciplinary hearing a couple of months ago, but I'm sure my brain isn't just inserting his face into the picture out of some kind of subconscious malice. I'm not crazy. I'm fine.

Oh, I've completely made my peace with the hearing situation too, don't worry about that. I seem to recall being quite cross at the time, but there's nothing to be gained from letting these things niggle away at you. I'm reasonably confident that I was wronged, so if there's some sort of tabulation when you die then it'll all be chalked up on the positive side of the ledger, presumably.

They'd announced that we were moving offices, you see. I wasn't overly keen on the idea, having worked there for twelve years and grown quite attached to the building, or at least to the routine, so I affected a wry anti-office-move stance, which didn't really gain any traction as my colleagues are all young and trendy and were pretty keen to move to the new premises as it's a lot closer to all the fashionable bars. When I pointed out to HR that my travel costs would be going up, given that the new place was in Zone 1 rather than Zone 2, they sent a terse email back saying that there would be no compensation for such a thing as the office was 'still in London', and maybe I should consider the cycle-to-work scheme. This amused me, as cycling to the new office from my house would take a couple of hours each way, and frankly that was more effort than I was willing to put in, it very much goes against my routine of beer and cake to suddenly be a lycra-toting cycleperson, so I screengrabbed the email, along with a Google Maps screengrab showing the route, and stuck it on Facebook as a comical off-the-cuff observation of corporate nonsense, for all of my many (er, twenty-two) online chums to share in the bechortling of.

Naturally, as anyone familiar with the ins-and-outs of my personal fate and fortune could have deduced, this post was immediately shared with HR by a colleague and flagged as 'not acting in the best interests of the company', 'a contravention of social media policy', 'possible gross misconduct' and all sorts of other things which I was rather revolted by at the time but obviously am completely fine with now, I mean, time heals all wounds and so on, and nobody ever died from having a meeting.

Disciplinary hearings are not fun, it has to be said, it's like being in court, having to defend yourself to your bosses against each individual charge. Still, I think Jed derived some amused pleasure from it, so there's a positive of sorts to be drawn there. Every cloud. Good for him, he's climbing that ladder.

Pictures of torn and broken bodies circulating around the internal office social channels help to break up the routine of the rest of the day, although I'd suggest that these images don't quite carry the gravitas of actually being able to smell the blood and hear the shell casings ricocheting off the venerable bridge's mighty structure and plopping down into the Thames. But again, I keep my mouth shut, because I'm sure they don't want to talk to me about it, that's fine, from that perspective this is just another day in our respective lives and I'll just keep myself to myself. It's reassuring to note that my lunch has been stolen from the fridge and my computer is playing up, leading me to spend ninety minutes on the phone with IT while my stomach rumbles extravagantly. The normality of all this is delicious.

Stepping down from the train at Stoneleigh – an hour later than expected, thanks to an unspecified track fault that gave me plenty of time to get into my book and thus shall be harboured no ill will – I'm struck by the really quite complex arrangement of aromas which greets alighting passengers. You'd think that having one of the highest rates of council tax in the country might mean that the council would organise for the bins to be emptied occasionally, but you have to admire their belligerent refusal to do so, it shows a strength of character and a fortitude that's so lacking in society these days. It's not the smell of pungently decomposing refuse, it's the smell of wealthy men in nice offices living by their own code, and that's good for them as they have expensive houses to maintain and green fees to cover and mistresses to extravagantly appease, as this is one of the perennial constants of society which reassures us that everyone has their own place.

Headphones in situ, I allow my ears to take over since my nose is temporarily annoyed, although a certain further aggravation occurs when the iPod's shuffle function decides to serve up a Lostprophets track as an opener, because of course you can't listen to that any more, it's tainted by the revoltingness, and then I don't really notice the next couple of songs because I'm busy concentrating on not being annoyed by the first one, but then Elliott Smith saunters in to pour oil on the acoustic waters and it washes over in an awesome wave, because everything works out alright in the end, doesn't it? I mean, it didn't for him, but I try very hard not be influenced by that. I try. And I'm sufficiently relaxed by the time I arrive home that the police car outside isn't cause for alarm. A quick mental check to ensure that I haven't done anything wrong that I can think of, and I'm released to pop the headphones back in my leather satchel, which really has been doing sterling service these last couple of years, really a pleasure to use, and the necessary safety pins now holding the strap in place lend the old-timey leather an intriguing retro punk frisson, and I nonchalantly slip the key into the door and unroll a pitch-perfect and entirely casual 'Oh, hello officer' as the bobby in question approaches.

We've reached the how-do-you-take-it stage of the tea process before the penny drops, and it becomes screamingly obvious to me that this particular policeman is the same one who spoke to me on the bridge yesterday. Wilson. I'm not totally sure I remember giving him my details, although I suppose it's entirely possible that he traced back a digital breadcrumb trail from my 999 call or something, the details of his arrival strategy seem redundant given that he's already here, so there appears to be little point asking. He sits at the kitchen table and I hand him a mug of tea, boldly decorated with a big Rolling Stones tongue which I've always felt has acted as a decent accompaniment to the inherent natural mouthwatering that an anticipated hot beverage brings forth, already realising that he asked for 'one sugar, quite milky' and I've erroneously provided 'two sugars, not quite enough milk'. This kind of tea anomaly can cause friction, but I've ceased to let such things irk me and can only assume that, as a professional, his position on the receiving end

will be one of tact. I don't imagine it's an arrestable offence.
Oh wait, no, he rang didn't he? He rang last night. That's why
he's here. Got it.

I sit opposite him, and he opens his notebook. I notice that his
nice pen is demonstrably absent. But a lot of people lost things
yesterday, it's probably impolite to point out the rubbishness of
his biro.

He has a penetrating stare, almost as if he's looking through me
to the windowsill behind, and I wonder whether he's judging me
for the brown edges of the leaves on my peace lily. It's a robustly
bushy plant, I'm quite pleased with how it's getting along,
although it is infuriatingly sensitive to water. Some days I give it
too much and it sits there, saturating in an almost belligerent
manner in a pool of brackish yellow soup; other days I realise I
haven't watered it for a while as its leaves theatrically wilt, like a
teenager trying to make a point about how unfair everything is.
Wilson begins eyeing me in a slightly suspicious way, and it
occurs with troubling awkwardness that, once again, I haven't
been listening to him and he's actually been talking to me for
some time. I take a sip of my tea, which is a mistake as it's still far
too hot and it makes my tongue do that extravagantly burny
thing which feels like too much punishment for too little crime,
and attempt to collect myself.

"I'm sorry, it's been a bit of a day. What was that?"

"I was merely outlining, sir, the reason for my presence here
today. Witness statements are often taken in police stations, as
you may be aware from the television dramas and such, but
given the sensitive nature of the happenstances yesterday and
the potential for mental trauma I felt it more apposite to question
you in your own home."

What an odd thing to say. Do they get taught to talk like this at
police school?

He takes a sip of extremely hot tea, and doesn't even flinch
slightly. "Forgive me, I don't mean 'question you' per se," he
continues. "Merely probe you for info, as it were."

Well, it's been a while since anyone was probed in this kitchen,
although I bite my scalded tongue before ejaculating this ribald
retort as it may well not be appropriate to the mood. So I settle
for: "Certainly, officer."

"Detective Chief Inspector, actually."

"Right."

"Although Brian is fine."

Having sidled crab-like to the fridge for a fuller injection of milk, my tea has now cooled sufficiently for me to take a heartier gulp as I ponder this new information. His name is actually Brian Wilson? He must have had a hell of a time at school. Maybe that's why he became a policeman. I suppose Brian isn't that uncommon a name for a man of his age, and Wilson certainly isn't unusual. The likelihood of these monikers juxtaposing isn't outside the realms of possibility.

I can't think of anything to say to him that isn't about the Beach Boys, but thankfully his rank and presence ensure that he's qualified to take the reins of the conversation, and this now demonstrates itself to be the case.

"I shan't keep you too long," he says, "as I imagine you're a little shaken up."

"No... no, really, I'm..."

"So we'll just dive right into it, shall we? First of all, can you tell me about your journey along the bridge yesterday, in your own words?"

He really is an odd fellow. My own words. Who else's words does he think I'm going to attempt to commandeer? But I suppose this is all just more of the necessary jargon of police work and it would be needlessly harsh to begrudge him the ingrained speech patterns of his respected profession, so I simply lay the facts of the situation out on the figurative table, being careful not to garnish with needless embellishment because hey, he's a busy man, he probably has other witnesses to talk to. Or 'question'. Or whatever.

Wilson's points of conversation follow the predictable textbook lines of myriad movie scenarios – did I know anyone there? Was it my first instinct to hide or run? What's my general view on terror attacks? – all seemingly chasing one answer while aiming to deliver quite another, but frankly the idea of overthinking any of it feels like wearisome effort and I have nothing to hide and I really just want an ice cube to put on my tongue because it's starting to smart quite unacceptably and has the potential to put a crimp on dinner.

"...and finally we come to your mood at the moment I approached you on the bridge."

"My mood?"

"Yes, sir. Your mood. Do you remember the question I asked

you?"

"Er... no. No, not really. There was a lot going on."

"Of course." He looks as if he's on the cusp of elaborating but thinks better of it. "Well, you've been more than helpful sir, and I hope you don't mind if there are a few follow-up questions in the near future, once I've chased up these lines of enquiry?"

I have no idea which lines of enquiry he's referring to as I got distracted by wondering what Wilson had done with his nice pen and whether he was the sort of person who'd proffer it up to use a makeshift splint or something, or perhaps if it had just slipped down into the gap beside the side bolster of his squad car's driving seat, but he's clearly keen to get on with the evening so I offer a cheery "Fine, fine" and show him to the door.

He's looking at me very strangely, but there's every chance that he looks at everyone this way, so he'll find no judgement in these quarters. You can't help what your face looks like, and our unique intricacies and idiosyncrasies are what make us all special little snowflakes and our mothers love us. Godspeed and adieu, officer. Sorry, Detective Chief Inspector.

Finding myself uncharacteristically not hungry, I decide to retire to the living room and sit for a bit, which is great because I love a good sit and the world really would benefit from a decent amount more sitting. The wallpaper, which was there when we moved in and had been there for goodness knows how long beforehand, always draws the eye in an irresistible way, and I find myself staring into it for slightly too long until I feel like I can't escape the imagery of that Charlotte Perkins Gilman short story I had to read at university, so I take mum's urn off the mantelpiece and cradle it in the nook of my elbow as I lower myself back into the sofa, which really has worn in nicely on this side with the springs getting all pliant and welcoming, and click the TV on. Some sort of reality show about famous people on an island is flickering through the room and I have absolutely no idea (or interest) what the premise is, it's just very nice indeed to have a splash of escapist variety that I can comfortably ignore. The urn feels strangely warm as I cuddle it to the side of my chest, and that's probably something to do with the central heating, which I'm sure I switched off but I'm not a gas engineer so who knows what goes on with that thermostat, and the growing warmth of the urn echoes in the warmth within my heart. These are the good moments, the comfortable ones. The warmth is otherworldly.

Is the thing *actually* getting warmer? Quite possibly. I know as much about the thermal properties of porcelain (if, indeed, the urn *is* porcelain) as I do about the plumbing. It doesn't matter. It's just nice to cuddle up, isn't it?

Chapter Three

Epsom Downs looks very different on a sparkling June morning to how I remember it from the misty April Meeting I attended a few years ago, having won a ticket to the event at the local butcher's which had just opened and was holding a raffle, and has since closed down because people don't appreciate the merits of a decent butcher any more and would rather have an Ocado warehouse employee pick their sausages out for them. Indeed, the last race meeting I attended required spectators to stand behind a white metal barrier some distance from the track, as I recall, whereas today we're able to stand right up against the rather flimsy wooden fence with the horses whizzing past a mere arm's length away. Presumably they've had a redesign, who can say? I'm just happy to be out.

There's a freshness and clarity to the air, and a serenity that belies the colossal crowds in attendance and it takes me some time to attribute it to a lack of planes in the sky, which I imagine is down to some manner of air traffic control strike or what-have-you. Good for them, industrial action is a vital cog in the corporate machine, I hope they achieve what they want to achieve, although it is a shame for all those holidaymakers.

My double-breasted suit in brown tweed is a welcome break from the everyday jeans-and-t-shirt of office life and I feel distinctly dapper in my bowler hat and pocket square, none of which are garments I recall purchasing or even putting on but the mind is a funny thing and I must have bought them because here they are. So often in life anguish is caused by questioning things too much, and instead of picking through my personal history of sartorial investments I decide instead to simply accept the fact that I'm here and go and put a bet on. That's the point of Derby Day after all, is it not?

The bookie's vast Chesterfield overcoat has something of the Rodney Trotter about it, although a hazy footnote in my brain suggests that perhaps such a reference would fall on deaf ears, so instead I gaze at the race card while pretending to at least have some vague idea of what the hell I'm doing, and then pick a horse at random because, sod it, the odds are better than a scratchcard whichever one I choose. Craganour seems like a solid choice, as it feels like the sort of rugged Scottish name that could be depended upon, it sounds like a nice peaty single malt. I listen in on the chap in front of me placing a bet as I have no idea how much to spend, there really should be a beginners' handbook; then again, maybe novices deserve to lose their money, it fortifies the spirit and encourages you to learn and not act rashly, but the hubbub of the mêlée means I can't make it out, so I'm going to have to wing it.

"Hello," I say to the bookkeeper.

He looks bemused, as if salutations aren't part of his line of work. He leaves the pause a heartbeat too long, then says at extravagant length: "Well, hello to you, good sir. And how may I help you today?"

There's a strong chance that the posh accent is an affectation and he may well actually be taking the piss, but who am I to cast aspersions on people's diction? I myself have been described as 'annoyingly nasal' by a co-worker, to the agreement of several others – not to my face, naturally, but hiding around the corner of the office kitchen is a reasonable way of honestly gauging perception rather than letting folk lie to one's face, there's no denying that.

"Ah, yes, I'd like to place a bet on Craganour," I say, feeling a little like Bernard Black but, again, somehow aware that the reference would be lost on the present audience.

He seems pleased by this. "A fine choice, sir. Craganour is the favourite, on at 6-4. Firm ground today, perfect for his form."

I have absolutely no idea what this means; I can understand odds if they're set against a one, as the difference between 10-1 and 100-1 is pretty easy to deduce, but where's the bloody four come from? And surely firm ground would benefit every horse – or are there some nags which prefer to slosh around in mushy, swampy quagmires? It doesn't matter on the whole, clearly, as this particular horse is the favourite and I've inadvertently made an excellent decision. Better a small guaranteed win than a large risky loss. Or something. I'm out of my depth, I'll admit, but I'm already having a jolly nice time.

I've been silently (if not deliberately) eyeballing him for a few seconds now and he appears uncomfortable. Keen to move the transaction onward, he continues: "Well then, how much would sir like to place?"

He licks the tip of his pencil theatrically, and holds it aloft with a certain poise that would make for an excellent soap opera scene.

I consider telling him so but I don't wish to fawn, so I join in his enthusiasm for progressing the conversation.

"Er, a pound?"

"A *pound*?!"

"I… think so?"

He looks me up and down, as if assessing my social standing and fiscal liquidity, and the likelihood that I actually have any cash on me.

"Well, it's your money sir."

I'm taken aback by this response, I have to say, although the way his eyebrows have begun to dance across his furrowed brow is most satisfying. Is that too small a sum? I rifle through my pockets and find myself with a palmful of thick, weathered coins; farthings and ha'pennies mostly, with a couple of shillings. Ah yes, of course. That… makes sense? I *think* it does. Does it?

The bookie is evidently aware of a growing queue of punters behind me and, much as I hope he's been enjoying our little back-and-forth, hastens to arrive at an apposite solution.

"Shall we call it a shilling, sir?"

"What? Oh, yes… yes, of course. Thank you."

The ticket stub is in my hand in what feels like microseconds, and before I know it the tightening crowd is eddying and swirling me to its edge away from the trackside, which works out rather nicely as this is where the bar is and I'm suddenly very much in the mood to exchange coins for beverages and get the day going with a bit of a pop. I note with idle interest that I haven't yet spotted a sole person dicking about with a smartphone, which I guess can be attributed to some new policy by the management. Everyone's very smartly dressed with hats to match and there isn't a single neck tattoo in sight, and there's probably a reason for that, but the shiny row of bottles is now tantalisingly close so the dynamics and demographics of the crowd can analyse themselves as I have thirst-quenching business to attend to.

There's a lull at the bar as it seems that this is the ideal moment for everybody to be placing their bets, and it's almost as if the waiting time to do so has been exponentially increased by some dithering berk holding up the line, if you can picture such a thing, so I ask the barman, who's busy polishing glasses with a dirty rag and no doubt achieving something entirely counterproductive, for a recommendation.

A moment's scrutiny of my features and possible assessment of my general character suggests that he's considering something amusing. "Buddy," he leers, giving away his Americanness with two unmistakable and thoroughly un-Epsom-like syllables, "tell me somethin'. Do you enjoy the theatre?"

That's not really the answer I was expecting, and it takes a few seconds for the correct synapses to fire into formulating a response. The way he pronounced it 'thee-ay-derr' threw me, I've not heard that done before.

"Um…" Yep, classic response, top work.

"Because if you do, I'm sure y'all know about the Pink Lady?"

"Oh… it's a kind of apple, no?"

He delivers the derisory look I no doubt deserve, before again applying the Cheshire cat smile and exposing all of those many, many teeth.

"The Pink Lady, my man, is a fabulous musical comedy, the kind that gets 'em rollin' in the aisles. Know what I mean? A whirlwind of romance, philandering, idiot-savants, mushroom-pickin'…"

"Mushroom-picking?"

"…that so enraptured the crowds, it span off its own goddamn *cocktail*."

Aha. I suspect we'll presently be arriving at the point.

"The Pink Lady," he continues, with a rising tone that theatrically ensnares the ears of a number of other patrons, "is a cocktail that will go down in history. We're talkin' the finest gin, grenadine, and egg-white – and you know who makes the best goddamn Pink Lady in town?"

Well, Epsom Downs isn't really in the town, is it? It's sort of out in the countryside. But I think I know what he's getting at.

"You?"

"Me! My own special recipe: we start with the gin, grenadine and fresh egg-white, and I add three more things. One: lemon juice. Two: applejack. Except that you limeys don't seem to know what the hell that is, so I substitute it with gin. And three: more gin."

I like this guy. "Sold!" I cry, and we arrange the necessary transaction. In fact, I order two, because why the hell not? And with a fruity, eggy, inverted pyramid of puddingy gin in either hand, I make my way back trackside.

Elbowing your way through a crowd isn't easy when you're carrying volatile cocktails, so it seems prudent to neck the pair and squeeze through with arms tucked in, moshpit style, and sure enough a fresh opening appears right by the barrier just for me. A gorgeous little bit of serendipity. Tattenham Corner, the last curve before the home straight – it rings a bell for some reason that I can't quite put my finger on, and the crowd's thickening out by the second so it's clearly the place to be.

I seem to remember there being TV screens showing the action last time I was here, but there's no such luxury today, and the voice coming through the small conical PA speakers with its clipped received pronunciation sounds more like the narrative of a wartime movie reel than anything particularly ITV-like, but the realities of the situation are what they are and the gin's kicking in so everything's fine.

A woman with a steely look in her eyes has clearly been inspired by my elbows-in crowd penetration manoeuvre, and shuffles her way to the front of the throng, leaning her forearms on the barrier beside me. Perhaps she's been fortified by multi-gin cocktails too? She certainly seems a little agitated, the seriousness in her gaze somewhat counterpointed by a noticeable edginess. Ants in her pants, my mum would have called it. She's probably put a bet on too. I thumb through the race card, scouting for likely candidates. Yep, Aboyeur at 100-1, I bet that's what she's flung a shilling on. I consider asking, but it seems like the sort of question that might wind her up as she's clearly already agitated, so instead I take a moment to admire the scarf she's holding, folded neatly but grasped uncomfortably tightly in her right hand. A delicate cream affair, with thin purple and green stripes almost identical to my old school colours, which again I consider bringing up before concluding that this is false confidence inspired by gin and I should leave the poor woman alone because she's clearly got a lot on.

And so the race begins. The abrupt syllables bouncing around the conical speakers rise in tone to fever pitch as the plummy commentary unfurls the happenings of the race; Aboyeur takes an early lead (ooh, surprise, how Hollywood!), Craganour comes alongside to challenge on the straight (great!), Nimbus and Great Sport are thundering along at a lateral distance, Shogun, Louvois and Day Comet come up on the inside, Craganour bumps into Abeyour who veers toward the rail, impeding Shogun and Day

Comet's line, Abeyour and Craganour collide again, and there they are, they're storming past us around the curve, the ground shakes, the tingling scent of chlorophyll increases as the hooves mash the neatly manicured grass, the rush of air like a train exiting a tunnel thumps the chests of everyone alongside the railings, the steam of sweat from the horses' shimmering flanks is almost tangible, and the woman with the steely eyes slips under the barrier, standing in the wake of the pack as if unsure what to do next, and she holds the scarf up toward the King's horse, and the horse raises its hooves in confusion as if to attempt to jump her, and the woman is trampled under its mighty and unstoppable heft, and almost before its begun it's all over and the horses are away and there's nothing before us but an unravelled scarf and a crumpled and broken body.

The crowd remains dumbstruck for longer than feels strictly comfortable and I consider the possibility that they all feel as I do, rooted to the spot like an oak tree, roots so deep and intertwined that movement is impossible, before compassion prevails and people start to rush toward the body, mangled and inert, while a breakaway crowd encircle the scarf and absorb its motif, 'Votes for Women', with a terrifying quietness. The acid scent of blood in the air smells like Waterloo Bridge. And I can't, I can't be here, I can't, and my roots uproot and I push against the tide, forcing my way back through the crowd, past the Chesterfield overcoat and the gleaming American teeth and out toward the turnstile, over the rutted track dodging between shiny new Austins and bullnose Morrises and across the fields to anywhere, the chlorophyll rises, but it can't mask the smell of pennies, and all I see is purple and green.

Chapter Four

beep-beep-beep
beep-beep-beep
beep-beep-beep

Sounds which integrate into dreams are just the worst, as there's a solid chunk of time – which could be mere seconds or whole minutes, it's impossible to tell when you're asleep – during which I think the smoke alarm's going off, except that it's not a real smoke alarm but a cartoon drawing of one which is hovering around the room and fluttering away every time I get close to pressing the off button, and that means that I'm wasting my energy on trying to silence the alarm rather than actually dealing with the fire, before I realise that actually it's just my alarm clock beeping and everything's OK and there is no fire and no fluttering cartoon smoke alarm and it's just time to get up.

I glance at the time with my bloodshot and gin-tainted eyes, and wonder whether Lance, the extravagantly bearded account man I spoke to once and inexplicably never again, ever wonders where his alarm clock went after he left the company, and what he'd think if he knew I'd found it in an office cupboard a couple of years later and taken it home, and had in fact used it now for longer than he ever did so it was essentially more my clock than it was his by squatters' rights alone, and the minutes are ticking by and I should really crawl out of my pit or the whole commuting timetable will go to cock.

The thinning hallway carpet pokes at my feet with the gripper rods' sharp teeth as I make for the stairs, but that's alright and doesn't bother me any more as I'd weighed up the cost of recarpeting the hall and concluded that it wasn't worth it, since I was the only one who used it and the other carpets in the house are reasonably decent, and the corridor's dark and you can't see how threadbare it is anyway. I consider the nature of my fuzzy tongue as I stumble into the kitchen, wondering what exactly it was that created the illusion of fuzz, or indeed if it actually was some kind of cloying but ultimately soluble real fuzz, and flick the kettle on to commence the craft of the cure. Tea solves pretty much everything, mum always said, and never a truer word spoken. Like the day the paperboy was knocked off his bike outside and he was bleeding from all sorts of places, and mum made him a strong cuppa with oodles of sugar and it somehow fixed him until the ambulance arrived. In hindsight she might have put something else into it besides sugar, but the point stands that tea is the healer.

The scattered pieces of last night's jigsaw puzzle shuffle themselves into order as I glance around the clean but dishevelled arrangement of objects in the room. Mum's urn is sitting on the breakfast bar, and I quickly return it to the living room mantle before she notices or something – and then the kettle clicks and the neurons fire and the beverage assembly can commence; bag in mug, hot water, stir, leave, stir, squish, squish, squish, jettison bag, spoonful of sugar, another for good measure, hearty slug of whole milk, always whole because semi-skimmed feels like a compromise and skimmed isn't milk at all, it's basically just white water, and whole milk carries those memories of childhood, milk delivered to the doorstep in glass bottles, popping off the foil top, finding a thick slug of cream at the surface, the cereal-clogging reward for being first to the step. And the other puzzle pieces: the empty gin bottle in the recycling bin – had it been full before? That would be some achievement – and the erroneous copy of *Racing Post* that had been sitting on the doormat, completely inexplicably, as I have zero interest in horse racing and never have done, and the open and empty carton of eggs, and the gore-splattered pestle and mortar which looks utterly hideous but on closer investigation appears to be full of smashed up pomegranate pulp, and the cheesy plastic bowler hat from last Hallowe'en's misguided attempt to present a Jeeves-and-Wooster effort but with the notable absence of a Wooster.

I devour the hot tea in three slightly painful but ultimately rewarding gulps. There is little time to shilly-shally. Presumably the train will be bang on time this morning, they're due a spot of timetabling success and good on 'em, I'm rooting for them.

The excellent croissant from the bakery outside Stoneleigh station, which is buttery and soft and warm – the croissant, not the bakery, although that is also pleasingly warm, if not especially buttery, but nobody wants a buttery floor, that'd be asking for trouble – is a divine way to pass the thirty-five minute delay on the gracefully crumbling platform, and that's actually worked out OK as eating a croissant at your desk always results in endless crumb escapes which live forever in your keyboard and invariably also end up in your hair and down your trousers, and lead people with diminished capacities for humour to make xenophobic comments in 1970s-sitcom 'aw-hee-haw-hee-haw' accents, so the day's already off to a flying start.

This magnificent success continues on arrival at the office as I find that, in spite of clear precedent, my desk and its contents haven't been tampered with in any way and there's minimal arsing around before I can get into the swing of things, which may well be a direct karmic by-product of the evening gin that I apparently decided to embark upon despite the last thing I remember before the troubling equine episode being sitting on the sofa with mum and half-watching the TV, but then it becomes apparent that for the first time in forever my colleagues actually want to talk to me about something and I attempt to calculate whether this needs to suggest cause for concern. News footage of Waterloo Bridge is playing and replaying on the big screen at the end of the office as it has been since the first day of the aftermath, and one of the many colleagues whose names have forever slipped my mind because respect is a two-way street and I try, I really try, but there's a limit, is pointing at the screen and shouting "there, there he is." A gaggle of them crowd around me and sweep me toward the screen, and one of them ruffles my hair and says "Mate, there's you, that's you by the barrier, I'd recognise that shit Itchy & Scratchy t-shirt anywhere," and he's right, there I am in bright green for the CCTV to pick up with impressive clarity, and I wonder whether the contractors for that excellent barrier are also anything to do with surveillance because the picture really is top-notch and if I were selling security systems for public overpasses I'd definitely think about bundling them together like that, you'd make a killing, excuse the inappropriate turn of phrase.

Mate. An unexpected term, and one generally lacking from the office lexicon whenever I'm involved, which is fine as I don't expect these people to be friends, they're colleagues, they're younger and trendier and there's really no problem with us having differing interests and routines and lifestyles and perceptions of what constitutes humour, and it seems likely that it's merely a vocal tic rather than a genuinely inclusive term of companionship, although there is a pathetically desperate part of my brain that's enormously chuffed to be included in that potentially pivotal word.

"You never said you were on the fucking bridge!"

"No, I er..."

"Fuck me! Look, the gunman goes right past you, there he is!"

It seems unusual that they're showing the footage in full on daytime TV, doesn't it? People actually dying on camera? That's the modern world I suppose, and I guess that's alright because people would undoubtedly find the footage and share it on Twitter anyway so the BBC are merely a conduit to inevitability here and why shouldn't they be?

"Well, I couldn't actually see that bit, because..."

"That must have been fucking terrifying! Jesus. Jesus H *Christ*. Mate, you nearly died!"

Mate again. A more suspicious person would speculate that their fresh new interest in me was solely down to my appearance on that screen rather than any real awareness of their general day-to-day beastliness, although they're not beastly really I suppose, they're just getting on with their lives, you can't take a positive interest in everyone, it'd be exhausting, and I'm aware before I'm even halfway through this avenue of thought that this is obviously the case and there's no point being sarcastic to myself about it and hey, step outside of yourself, they're actually talking to you without making your soul hurt so let's just go with it and see what happens.

"Red Lion?"

Ah. I might have dipped out of the conversation for a moment there. "Huh? Sorry, what?"

"Red Lion, lunchtime? Buy you a pint you can tell us all about it?"

Oh, frabjous day! "Sure, that sounds great! I mean, you know, let's see how the morning goes, I know there's the figures coming in from Madrid this morning and then we've got to prepare for the Chicago thing ahead of the brainstorm, and that data analysis company's coming in to make some sort of point about synergy or fusion or somesuch, and..." and they've all gone some time ago and I'm just jabbering to myself in front of looped footage of my balled-up body almost being shot, but that's fine because they've asked me out to the pub and that's literally never happened before, and I'm so flummoxed by it that I've used the word 'literally' even though its modern overuse makes me shudder, although that is literally how language evolves, by common usage, so I'm completely comfortable with that.

The Red Lion is the sort of pub that really throws into sharp focus how much better it was going to the pub before the smoking ban, because back in the good old days pubs stank of stale smoke and fresh smoke and just general smoke, which wasn't great but at least it was a naturally pub-like aroma, whereas nowadays you can really smell the things that all the smoke was masking, which is old carpets saturated with stale beer and the effervescent body odour of the sort of people that turn up at the pub as soon as the doors open in the morning and remain there all day drinking pints of mild without ever considering the concept of rinsing their armpits once in a while, but I don't hold any grudge because I'm secretly rather jealous of the kind of lifestyle that would afford such freedom of the schedule. The table we're sitting at is reassuringly sticky, as all good pub tables should be, and the presence of salted peanuts is a gorgeous throwback to the memories of sitting in the little conservatory outside the village pub when I was a kid while mum was inside with her friends and occasionally popping out with a fresh Coke for me, and the relentless urban myths about the number of different types of urine found in pub peanuts does nothing to deter me from devouring them now as it tastes like eating the past. No-one else is here yet but that's entirely to be expected, I had a busy morning too, and I know they said one o'clock as a loose time-frame rather than setting anything in stone, so I'm nursing a pint and just waiting.

It's about 1:45 when they eventually appear and I wonder whether fifteen minutes is enough to tackle lunch as well as 'telling them all about it', but I see that Jed's here too and he's the decision-maker on timesheets and so on so perhaps there's a bit of leeway. They ruffle my hair in a world-first and set about ordering up a round on Jed's company credit card, which doesn't include me as I already have a pint but that's alright, it's probably not a good idea to drink all of the beer at lunchtime anyway, I don't need it, and I'm not affronted that they didn't even ask because I'm sure they logically assumed.

"Well," says the one who I think might be called Martin, fixing me with a pointed stare.

"Er...?"

"Tell us all about it. Your story. Your tale of besiegement and survival."

"OK. Um, sure. Well, I was walking toward the station, aiming for the 17:47 as usual because that's the train which gets me back into Surrey at a decent time to sort things out before I get the dinner on, although it's often running late so the plan doesn't always work out, but..."

A table full of blank looks and quizzical eyebrows is quite a pressuring thing. I can't help these words, they just tumble, it's always been that way and I've made my peace with it but it's a whole other thing which would take a lengthy explanation so perhaps I should just reorient myself with the point.

"...um, and anyway, as I was crossing the bridge I saw this car coming towards the barrier, really fast..."

"What kind of car?"

They know what kind of car. They've seen the footage a hundred times. I know piss all about cars and even I could identify what kind of car it was. Have I just sensed a shift in mood?

"A Focus. An old one, in a sort of watery shade of green." Silence, stares. I consider describing it further, the crinkly dent in the door and the incongruous National Trust sticker in the window, as that seems to be what they're after, detail, and perhaps I ought to proffer an analysis of, I think I remember rightly, the mould-breaking control-blade suspension the model was fitted with and the jarring nature of the New Edge design which really was a giant leap forward from the Escort it replaced, none of which means anything to me at all but there was an old copy of *Auto Express* in the dentist's waiting room a while back and I memorised this information for exactly this sort of occasion, although now the moment's come I'm not totally confident I've remembered it correctly, but I'm now so tied up in what they might want to hear that I've totally forgotten what I was saying and it seems that the one who might be Martin has been talking for some time.

"...the footage, you can see the moment when the crowd realise the gunman's a target himself and they surge up and overcome, it's proper fucking Van Damme. They just grab him, loads of them, his neck's at a weird angle and it's obvious he's snuffed it, and they just launch him into the river. Brutal." He laughs, he fucking laughs, like he's describing some fucking movie he's seen at the IMAX or something and it really isn't fine at all, *it isn't fine at all*, and I can't think of anything I'd like to do more than throw him in the fucking river, and I blurt out "Pennies!" Unsurprisingly, they all look taken aback.

"What?!"

"Er… pennies. The blood, it… smells like pennies. I'm sorry, I've just remembered I've got a conference call with the, um, those guys from, er…" and I'm out the door and up the street in a flash and immediately the gentle summer breeze washes over me and there's tweeting birds and jangling bicycle bells and whistling delivery drivers and it's fine, really, everything's fine.

They don't acknowledge me back at the office. The return to normality is incredibly refreshing.

The train home is running perfectly on time, and frankly I don't know what to do with that information, it almost feels like an act of sympathy. Wilson arrives while I'm cooking dinner, because of course he does, I'd forgotten that he'd rung to say he was coming back with a forensic artist and obviously the one time he'd be guaranteed to ring the doorbell would be when I'm elbows deep in lamb mince. One on-time train does not herald a shift in the fortunes of the cosmos.

Wilson introduces me to the artist, a chap named Kenny, as they walk into the kitchen, and as I invite them to take a seat I'm distracted by the thought that I don't think I've ever met a real Kenny before and my only frame of reference here is Kenny from *South Park*, who obviously relentlessly dies, and of course there's Kenny Everett, and Kenny Dalglish and Kenny Loggins, and Kenny Lynch and Kenny G, actually there's quite a few Kennies in the world. It seems like an improbable statistical anomaly that I've never crossed paths with one, and this particular one is looking slightly awkward now since I think I've been inadvertently staring at him a bit so I attempt to vocalise my findings on the subject of Kenny, much to his bemusement it seems.

"No, I can't say I've met a lot of other Kennies either."

Good, well that's cleared that up. I offer the two of them dinner out of politeness, since it seems a bit mad to finish cooking and eat by myself in front of them, and they surprise me by taking me up on the offer. Perks of the job, I suppose. Maybe they always call in on people at teatime, it must drastically reduce their grocery bills. It's not a problem really, as I'm making fajitas and there's too much for one person to eat anyway; not enough for three people as it stands, but it's the work of a moment to chop up another pepper and an onion and grate a load more cheese, that'll bulk it out.

"So I guess you want to create a photofit then?" I ask as I lay the various bowls out on the folding table, whose yellowing varnish is cracking and it was probably cheap when it was bought thirty-odd years ago but I don't want to get rid of it because it's where mum and I always used to eat together and it's something solid and tangible of hers to keep around.

"Well, not quite," says Kenny. "Photofits are made of photos." He holds his pencil aloft as if to demonstrate the fundamental difference in artistic approach, which is obvious when you think about it and now I can't look him in the eye because Jesus I'm a fool.

"We'd like you to describe the man as best you can," says Wilson, laying a paternal hand on my shoulder which catches me somewhat off guard, as strong male role models aren't exactly my thing and I have a tremendous urge to hug him and ask him questions about sport and girls and maybe boys too and woodwork.

"But... and tell me if I'm wrong, I don't want to tell you your job... isn't that a bit... pointless? I mean, you know who the gunman is, you dragged him out of the river. Plus he's dead. Why do you need a photofit – sorry, sketch – to identify him?"

"My apologies, sir, I thought I'd explained," Wilson oozes, like warm honey, and he most probably did explain, I do misplace things sometimes. "The *other* man – the driver. He's the one we're after. He escaped on foot and as you can imagine we're rather keen to track him down."

"Oh. Yes, of course. Well, I only saw him briefly as the car went past, just a glimpse. I was distracted by the man with the gun."

"Naturally. But anything you can tell us is useful, sir. Anything at all."

I methodically assemble myself a fajita, piecing it together in the only logical way: tortilla laid flat, spread of salsa covering the centre of the top two-thirds, then a spoonful of the spicy fried lamb mince/red onion combo, followed by a handful of grated cheddar, with a further handful of shredded iceberg lettuce on top, and a glob of sour cream as the final embellishment. Roll it into a cylinder, fold the empty bottom-third up and around, and try to eat it with as little mess as possible because there's a policeman and a Kenny looking, which turns out to be impossible, and a gooey dribble of tomatoey cream ambles through my stubble as I say "OK, well, he had a beard, I'm sure of that. A neat one, the kind where he's touched in his cheeks and neck-beard with a razor and kept the whole thing tidily short. Biggish eyes, slightly too close together. Longish nose, straight, quite pronounced. Um… he had a bit of a recede on, but no grey, just dark brown hair, shortish and straight."

They seem pleased with this level of detail, presumably given my initial pessimism of having only caught a glimpse, and I realise that I've actually been perfectly describing Jed from the office. Now that I think about it, I cannot picture the driver of the car at all; at least, not as anyone other than Jed. The images of the two have become one. But I can only assume he really did look like Jed, because memories are essentially all you have in this world and I can't bear the idea that my memory might be lying to me, that'd be terrifying.

I gesture to Wilson and Kenny to help themselves to another fajita as I ponder the reality of a possible false memory. I certainly don't think it actually *was* Jed driving the car, that would be weird, but it certainly could have been someone Jed-*like*. I realise at this point that I haven't offered either of them a drink and the fajitas are quite spicy and they've clearly been too polite to bring it up, and all I have is beer which I imagine they'd refuse as they're on duty or flat Coke which I can't think they'd want so I just get three pints of water and that's another achievement ticked off the to-do list, super.

Kenny lets me see the picture as I'm showing them to the door, and yes – it does look exactly like Jed. He's quite some talent, this fella. Alright, I've described the wrong person, but he's drawn an uncanny likeness of that person and he really is earning his money today.

As they leave, I'm secretly hoping that Wilson will turn around Columbo-style with a *'Just one thing…'* wagging finger, and I'm overjoyed when he does and can't help feeling that I somehow willed it into happening. But life can be serendipitous sometimes. It's what makes it so engaging.

"May I just ask you one more thing, sir?"

"Of course!"

"It's about your mother."

"…"

"Well, I assume she's your mother. The photo on the bookshelf in the hallway there? She looks like someone I knew, long ago. Viv. A nurse, down at St. George's?"

"That's right, that's her!"

"Yes, she, er… she helped me once. Is she around? I'd love to say hello."

"She's dead."

"Oh…"

"I mean, she is around, she's in an urn in the living room, although it might be a little fruitless to say hello, owing to the fact that she passed away last year."

"Oh, I am sorry. My apologies, I had no idea."

"Of course, there was no way you could know."

"No. Please, I…"

"Think nothing of it. I have to get on now, time waits for no man and all that, there are things to be and places to do and…" and I can still feel his eyes on me as I close the door, gently but firmly, and I sit down on the floor for a bit, hugging my knees and thinking about the last time someone said her name aloud. You don't really think of your mum having a first name, do you? After what could be minutes or a lifetime I get up and clear away the dinner things, pondering the overly diminished food quantities in the fridge which is obviously OK because it's nice to have company and these are the inherent sacrifices, and I knock the top off a beer and vacate the kitchen because the idea of the Jed likeness suddenly feels a bit awkward.

Mum's picture is mounted in a beautiful silver frame, one of the few truly valuable things in the house and I have no idea where it came from, and her eyes smile out from beneath a broad-brimmed hat, sparkling and radiant, the eyes I mean, not the hat, and she's arm-in-arm with someone in a grey herringbone suit but you can only see the arm so who knows who that might be.

She's looking slightly downward in the photo, which I assume must have been taken at somebody's wedding as she wasn't normally a hat enthusiast, and following her gaze onto the bookshelf I see the race card and the ticket stub. Craganour, one shilling. June 4th 1913. Right there next to my keys, like the most normal thing in the world.

I pick up the race card and turn it over in my hands. It has the slightly coarse, fibrous feel of vintage paper, and yet it doesn't feel like it's over a century old. It feels… well, like it was brand new yesterday. Which of course it was. But…

The insistent tick-tock of the hall clock has always had a mollifying effect, stretching and compacting time to its own whims, and there have been quite enough episodes of me loitering in the hall for confusingly indeterminate periods of time today, so I grab my no-longer-cold beer and settle myself into the sofa. I just, I don't…

I flick on the TV, and it settles reassuringly into the latest instalment of whatever the hell this celebrity reality thingy is. Apparently the key is to stay on the island and couple up and garishly procreate rather than attempt to escape the island, which I suspect would make for a rather more entertaining show, although I know very little about the intricacies of television scripting or commissioning and this is why other people do this job. It continues to be aired so there must be something in it. People like what they like. Maybe seeing celebs drowning as their home-made rafts sink wouldn't be a ratings winner.

I cradle the urn, and attempt to reset my mind to a state of perfect unclutteredness, as the vessel warms, as if to soothe. Like a hot water bottle for the soul.

Chapter Five

"Don't mind if I do, Gus." He hands me a dewy-cool bottle of beer from the small fridge he keeps secreted under the counter for these relentlessly hot summer days. The air conditioner in the shop packed up a couple of weeks ago and there's only so much you can do with a rotating fan, in this sort of heat and humidity you're basically just blowing hot air around the place and it's like being unpleasantly awoken by a dog panting hot breath onto your face. I imagine. Never been a dog person, but it's a very Hollywood motif isn't it?

I've been coming here for years – I think? – and Gus and I have a little back-and-forth going now. I bring him the afternoon papers and a little tray of Marshmallow Peeps, or maybe some Pepperidge Farm cookies, on my way uptown; in return, he slings me a Pepsi and we chew the fat over something and nothing. Since the air conditioner gave up the ghost, he's started stocking the fridge with Ballantine IPA or Rheingold, and I'm totally on board with that, it feels like a pretty decent reward for having to deal with the cloying heat of the Alabama summertime without any sort of airborne refrigerant.

I'm particularly pleased to be in the shop today, not just for the cold beer although that is pretty much the best thing that's happened so far, but for the fact that I suspect I'm about to make Gus very happy indeed. You see, today I think I might actually buy the Radiola.

"What kind of signal do you think it sends out to the customers, being an electrical goods store with a busted air conditioner?"

"You go fuck yourself, fella."

"No, really – d'you think they're likely to come inside and think *'Hey, his own hardware's crapped out on him and he can't get it fixed, but I'm sure all the rest of these optimistically-priced wares are fine and dandy'*?"

"I refer you to my previous advice. Drink your drink, there's a good boy."

He rolls up the *Montgomery Advertiser* and holds it aloft, smiling but with that trademark threat of malice playing about the smoker's wrinkles around the corners of his mouth, and waits for the fat little fly that's buzzing around the store to land somewhere that won't be expensive to batter it onto. Presently, as if scripted, its bulky black body lowers itself to the peeling brown Formica of the counter. Gus considers the fly for a moment, craning his neck and moving his head from side to side as if to assess the optimal angle of attack, before bringing the *Advertiser* crashing down to where the fly had been a couple of microseconds before.

"Shit."

I take a swig in sympathetic agreement, and the buzzing resumes near the wide-open door. Flies, of course, are too stupid to effect their egress through a convenient exit however helpfully they may be presented, and the chunky little buzzbox flutters itself onto the body of the defunct air conditioner. This, to Gus, appears to be the coalescence of all that's wrong with the world, or at least in his own particular microcosm, and he leaps over the counter – rather balletically, I feel – and crosses the floor in three strides, bringing the newspaper home in one vast and muscular arc that leaves the ex-fly smeared artfully across the steel like something you'd see in the Tate Modern. Although this feels for some reason like it might be a confusing reference to bring up, I can't quite pinpoint why, like I've just fabricated a pinprick of a future hypothetical, so instead I suggest that in a perfect world this killer blow would have encouraged the air conditioner to cough back into life, thereby killing two birds with one stone. Or rather, one fly with one newspaper, plus a fringe benefit. Gus is not amused by this. But serenity descends as he reinstalls himself behind the counter and resumes his pursuit of the bottom of the beer bottle. That's always a good place to be on a day like this.

Today. Today's the day I'm going to buy the Radiola, for sure. "Got that air conditioner working yet?" I smirk, as I drop the papers and the cookies on the counter. Gus's eyes briefly flit to the 'Christmas bargains' banner in the window before deeming my fatuousness too base to proffer a response to. There's a pan of water on the hotplate on the counter and he lights it with a thick match, manfully struck on the sole of his shoe which suggests to me that he's finally been to see *Fort Yuma* at the pictures like he's been talking about for the past few weeks, although I don't ask him about that as he's bound to bring it up anyway and I can't really get on board with Peter Graves, I think he'd be better suited to comedy than Westerns. Gus opens a tub of coffee while

I unhook a couple of tin mugs from the shelf above the counter.
"Any milk in that little fridge?"

"Yes *sir*, finest damn milk in the state. Pop Larson brings it in when he comes by on Tuesdays. Oo-*ee*, if his cows don't produce the creamiest sumbitch milk money can buy!"

"Yeah, except you don't buy it. Wait – you… you have other friends? Other townfolks come visiting the store to chew the cud? I thought I was the only one."

He smiles broadly as the water bubbles.

"Do you ever actually sell any of this shit, or are you just operating some kind of community outreach centre?"

"Well you tell me son, you sure as hell never bought nothin'."

He's got me there.

The spoon he uses to stir the coffee is like the sort of instrument you'd find in a garage, teaspoons that never get washed and form their own waxy brown protective coating. The kind of thing that can't infect you because its germs are too busy fighting each other.

"I was meaning to talk to you about that actually…"

"Y'all see this?" he cuts me off, gesturing toward the newspaper. "Goddamn commies trying to claim the Antarctic for their own!"

The headline reads '*Somov leads Soviet Antarctic Expedition*'.

"They're building some kind of lab, aren't they? A facility for experiments and observations."

"You believe that? Is that what you believe? Oh *my*."

"I sincerely doubt they're trying to claim the Antarctic as their own. What would be the point?"

"You kiddin' me? They love snow, they'll be right at home. Probably going up there to fuck some penguins before aiming some goddamn long-range missiles at us."

"Down."

"Huh?"

"Not up, down. Antarctica's the one at the bottom."

"You sure 'bout that?"

"They do have a lot of penguins down there though."

I walk over to the three-tiered shelf of radio sets, sipping my coffee which is so absurdly strong you could stand a spoon up in it, although with Gus's wretched spoon it probably has the sticky ability to stand up by itself anyway, and I decide to take the plunge. I've been saving, the money's ready, and I can't face the tension any longer. I'm doing it. It's happening.

"Gus, I'd like to take advantage of your generous pre-Christmas discounts."

An extravagant pause. "You don't mean…"

"Yup. I'm going to buy the Radiola."

He's momentarily dumbstruck. "Well, hot damn…"

The time is clearly right, it's last year's model so Gus will be able to sweeten a little discount from the supplier, and the yearning's becoming too much to bear. Those digits have been burned into my mind for twelve months now: RA364A. Ever since I heard that song *Hey Hey, It's OK,* it's meant everything, it just makes everything make sense, *'your life, ooh, it may be a dream'*, and I knew from the second I heard it that I'd have to buy myself a decent radio to hear it again in perfect clarity. And it had to be a Radiola, Gus had been chewing my ear off for years about this cutting-edge French technology. "You don't see a lot of 'em in these parts," he'd say, "but I know a guy…"

Through the sweltering summer afternoons and balmy autumn evenings to the brisk winter mornings, he'd evangelise about this company, Radiotechnique, extravagantly stretching the last syllable, who make the best tubes in the goddamn world, the crystal-clear quality, and all of this precision technology housed in strong modern plastics, no Bakelite, no cheap shit, buddy. The RA364A, that was the one to have – six tubes of superheterodyne splendour, low profile but big sound. Those doo-wop boys would never sound grander.

The look on his face is one of wonder as he fills out my details in the order book, handing me a carbon copy after I've scrawled my looping signature at the bottom with his Parker Jotter ballpoint, a seemingly incredible extravagance for a man who doesn't seem to sell much. I note with interest that my receipt is no.00042. That's not a big number. He must have paid four dollars for that pen, maybe five. Priorities, huh?

"I'll talk to my guy this afternoon, should have that shiny Radiola to you early next week," he grins, a classic Gus grin, eyes crinkling at the corners. "You got a phone number? Here, write it down for me, I can let you know when it's in."

"Aw, Gus, I'll know when it's in," I smile. I shake my friend's hand, button up my quilted Gabardine and step out into the crisp December evening.

Back in the autumn I was happy to walk the forty-five minutes or so from Centennial Hill to Cloverdale-Idlewild, but the wind is bitter today so it seems like a better idea to get the bus, even though the buzz of the Radiola is still enough to warm my palms; my face has other ideas, freezing itself into a rictus grin as I walk to the bus stop, stooping forward slightly against the icy breeze.

The bread-loaf GM is hovering at the lights a few blocks up as I round the corner of Washington and McDonough, so I scurry to the stop while frantically checking my pockets for dimes. Happily there's a City Lines transport token in my top pocket – I have no idea how it got there but it's good for a ride home, and as the bus heaves to the kerb with a pneumatic sigh, the doors concertinaing open with a rattle and a squeak (I don't why they do this, but every single Montgomery bus's doors seem to make the same slightly broken-sounding noise, rattle-rattle-click-squeak-rattle), I have the token in hand in the nick of time, dropping it to the driver and taking a seat near the middle. It's a comfortable place to be, square between the axles and ahead of the rear doors, and my mind wanders as the lights of the darkening downtown flash by. *'Your life, ooh, it may be a dream...'* I read something in the *Advertiser* that said *Hey Hey, It's OK* was the first rock 'n' roll record to reach the top ten in the pop charts, although I have to admit I don't totally understand the nuances of the definitions. Is doo-wop a form of rock 'n' roll? All I know is I can't get enough of that song. I just cannot wait to hear it oozing warmly from my very own Radiola. *'Hey hey, baby it's OK.'*

The seats have been gradually filling as we cross downtown, men and women in office attire making their way wearily home to sit in front of their fireplaces and tune in their own inferior domestic radio sets to the minstrels of the moment. As we cross the junction at Dexter I realise I've somehow got on the wrong damn bus, this isn't heading south in any sort of logical way at all, although I guess if we're going down Montgomery Street then I'll sort of be off in the right direction so that's alright, might as well stick with it. It's nice and toasty on here anyway, all these bodies breathing their warm condensation onto the windows. The bus stops outside the Empire Theater, and as the doors rattle and squeak shut the driver stomps down the aisle radiating vibes of mildly aggrieved displeasure. "There's white folks standin'," he grunts, moving the 'Colored Section' sign back a row and waving at four black passengers to get up. "Y'all better make it light on yourselves and let me have those seats." Three of them get up immediately, but one remains, simply shifting along to the window seat, a smartly-dressed lady with eyeglasses and a look of pure determination, the sort of look worn by someone who's already had a bit of a day and enough's enough, thank you.

"Go on, git," growls the driver, a menacing sonofabitch who seems intent on creating problems for himself. There were three white passengers standing. They've now been swapped for three black passengers in a zero-sum exchange of matter; not in any way fair but that's Alabama for you. Surely he wants to just make it to the end of his shift so he can go and warm himself by the fire and listen to the radio. Why make trouble and stress for himself? It's just another winter's day.

But the bee in his bonnet isn't simply about one woman's disobedience, that's obvious to everyone as the tension palpably rises, this is a race thing, an us-and-them standoff, there's no possibility of a little live-and-let-live decency here, he's been defied on his own bus and he won't stand for it, and he yells "Why don't you stand up?!" and she calmly replies "I don't think I should have to stand up", which sounds fair enough to me but plainly not to everyone at the front of the bus who are having their journey rudely disrupted by this impertinent negro and they really just want to get home to the fire. And then the driver, the *goddamn* driver, he storms to the front of the bus and shuts off the engine, and he rattle-squeaks open the door and hops off over to the phone box because we're outside the Empire and of course there's phones there, and he calls the police and sounds apoplectic as he unfolds the details of the situation down the line, and all the while she's sitting there looking dignified and serious and perhaps slightly scared which is more than understandable, and the folks at the front are muttering "I don't understand why that bitch won't move, them's the rules ain't they?" and "My supper's gon' be ruined" and "They're always impertinent, these folks, it's their fuckin' nature", and we just have to sit there in the growing chill until a police cruiser appears alongside, cherries ablaze, all panda and chrome in the dark, and the officer's grabbing her by the arm and she's saying "Why do you push us around?" and he's saying "I don't know, but the law's the law and you're under arrest," and she's off the bus and the engine clatters back into life and we're away down Montgomery Street and if it loops back toward the Garden District then I may well be back on the right track to Idlewild. *'Ooh, your life, ooh, it may be a dream, hey hey, baby it's OK, just let it all go and float away…'*

Chapter Six

"Can I have a word?"
The question rattles around my brain as I consider the possibilities. I mean, realistically, that's never good is it, coming from senior management? Jed and I don't exactly have a matey nicey-nicey relationship; sure, he acts all friendly when he needs to because that's his management style and while the easiest way up the greasy rope is to step on a few heads it doesn't hurt to smile while you're doing it, but we're not friends, especially after that *fucking* disciplinary, not that I'm bothered in the slightest about that now, it's all buried in the past and it's fine. No stress. I expended enough glucose on that. Christ, that's one of his terms, don't start talking like him, the glucose thing is meaningless, I bet he learnt it at a management conference, but I guess if he's comfortable talking like that then good for him, he's certainly doing well for himself. Everything's cool.
Everything's certainly very cool in the shower this morning, the boiler's doing that thing again, and I can't really afford to fix it but it's summertime and a nice cool shower is probably a healthy way to start the day. I can save up some money and worry about it in the winter. Well, not worry about it, that's not me, I mean it's just something to consider. And isn't 'warmduscher' the German word for wimp? Literally meaning someone who only takes warm showers? You learnt enough about wimpiness as a kid to not fear the cold. C'mon.

The fruit 'n' fibre is almost forming a caricature of Jed's face in the bowl, or at least his beard. Banana eyes. If I swish the spoon a little, I could send over a hazelnut nose. *"Can I have a word?"* It is making me a bit edgy, I'll admit, and I really don't enjoy uncertainties, I like to tick things off and move on to the next thing, having worries hanging over you is a burden of the way life used to be, it doesn't help you to worry about stuff. Maybe it's a pay rise, or a promotion? Why does it have to be something negative? Stop winding yourself up. It's OK, I'm sure everything's OK. Catch up with him first thing when you get into the office. And you can have a proper cup of tea when you get there, and there's nothing to be gained from beating yourself up about having let yourself run out of teabags here, the decaf ones for guests are by their very nature inferior but it's better than no tea at all, and you'll be in the office in ninety minutes' time anyway, trains permitting.

I had thought it had seemed a little lighter in the kitchen this morning, and as I step outside the front door I realise that this is because the car's disappeared, presumably it has been stolen as I'm the only one with a key or any claim to it, which explains why more sunlight was able to reach the window. It's the nature of having a driveway that leads right up to your kitchen, you inevitably have to eat while essentially sitting right next to your car, albeit with a few inches of exterior masonry between you. It's slightly gobsmacking, as I'm sure I should have heard it being removed, they can't have started it up to drive it away, they must have pushed it away or put it on a trailer or something. I very rarely use the thing so I suppose it's not the end of the world, I mean I get the train to work and I basically don't have anywhere to go or anything to do at the weekends so arguably I don't *need* a car, but it was mine and it was worth something and *fuck it all* and I'm sitting here on the drive with my arms around my knees shaking with a whole variety of emotions just like I was in the hall last night and it's fine, get up, it's important to get to the office because there's *"a word"* to be had and I dust myself off and subtract the car from present reality. It's not strictly part of the routine so I'll think about it later. I'm already two minutes behind my getting-to-the-station schedule so I have to walk in fast-motion like an old 1920s newsreel, and I need to be at the Kingston bypass by a quarter to eight in order to be at the end of Stoneleigh Park Road at ten-to, giving me a decent buffer of time to make it to the far end of the platform to be sitting at the front of the 07:57. Ha! Sitting? No, even in half-term that's a remote contingency. But there's always hope. Although if I'm going to meet my quarter-to marker at the bypass then I'll need to be exiting the end of the alleyway by the school no later than twenty-to and that's only a minute away and *oh my goodness I'd better run* and the schoolkids coming the other way always laugh at you when you run but they presumably don't have a Jed to deal with so I'll take the hit, thanks.

It's a little after ten when I finally, and sweatily, tumble into the office, thanks to an inexplicable period of waiting in a hermetically sealed and roasting train just outside Wimbledon for what seemed like an incredible amount of time, although I'm really enjoying re-reading Wodehouse at the moment, so I was able to reacquaint myself with Bertie and his man's sojourn to New York City as the furious commuters sandwiching their pungent armpittery around me grew increasingly vocal about the absence of toilets on commuter trains and the logistical possibilities of relieving themselves in water bottles without causing offence (or offensive splashing) to fellow travellers. Thankfully as far as the clock is concerned, Waterloo Bridge is now open to pedestrians, which scythed a decent chunk off the expected walking time, and the massively heightened police presence and cartoonishly large floral tributes and memorial banners lent the whole scene a jovial carnival atmosphere. Although that's obviously not the sort of thing you can say out loud; although again, having seen events unfold first-hand I'm probably more qualified to comment than most, but it's fine, I'll keep myself to myself as that's always the best way. Hush now. No-one wants to hear from you.

"…absolutely no fucking idea, he just legged it, he's so weird…" is cut off to nothing as I walk around the corner to the office kitchen, and to be fair they could have been talking about anyone, maybe they were discussing last night's football match if there was one, and I'm immensely relieved to find that the teabag jar runneth over and I'm able to make my first proper cuppa of the morning. Jed is among the group in the kitchen, now silenced like guilty teenagers and opening and closing their mouths in the style of the guppy as they try to quickly manhandle a new topic of conversation into place, but that's alright, we all get awkward. I tell Jed that I saw his email and am keen for the highlighted word to be had.
"How's right now?" he asks. Well, I have my tea so all is well in the world. I indicate that this is just dandy, and he directs me toward the meeting room across the way from the main entrance to the floor.
There is, it transpires, a minor disparity between our respective definitions of 'right now' as it takes him a good twenty minutes to join me, but this is actually quite a useful window of time with which to familiarise myself with the room as I've never actually

been in here before. I don't get invited to meetings. I ponder the peculiarity of the design, both of the room and of the building as a whole, as from where I'm sitting at the end of the conference table I can see not only the entire open-plan office floor through the glass wall, but also out through the main entrance door, which is glass, and through the entrance to the next-door office, which is also glass, as if there's no division between the two companies at all. This seems odd to me, and perhaps a cynic might speculate that the whole reason behind the office move, relocating to be within the same building as this other company, was to ultimately execute some kind of merger. But no, they'd promised us that no such thing would be happening before we moved over, and what reason could they have to lie to us?

The room fills with the smell of freshly incinerated nicotine as Jed sashays in, and I'm impressed with the level of easy confidence that he exudes because I'd probably feel a bit guilty about leaving someone waiting in a meeting room while I went off for a ciggie but I suppose the belligerent don't-give-a-fuckness of management grants you such freedoms.

"I won't beat about the bush, mate," he says, and I'm intrigued by the continued use of the word 'mate', I've never been one to say it much and the way everyone here starts throwing it into conversation when they want something from you feels somehow fraudulent, but I'm sure he's just being nice, he must have that capacity. "There's going to be a merger."

Well, fuck me sideways, is something I'd never say in a meeting with senior management no matter how delicious the sarcasm feels as I start to ball it up at the back of my tongue.

"Oh." Yep, that's really got him on the ropes.

"Yes, with Çalış & Çalış across the hall there. It's just obvious, isn't it? Same parent group, two agencies doing the same thing in the same building, it's mad not to bring them both under the same P&L."

I'm not sure if this is an appropriate time to bring up the fact that I've never totally understood what 'P&L' means, it's one of those buzzwordy business terms that gets thrown around in meetings and I've always just let wash over me, like 'tissue meeting' or 'let's put it to groups and share our learnings', and dammit I hate the word learnings, it's not a word, and Jed's eyeballing me now and expecting a response so I hit back once again with a solid and forthright "Oh".

"So the long and short of it is that we're letting you go, mate."

"…"

"Yeah."

"But… but I've been here twelve years. This is what I do."

"Sure, and we appreciate that, we do, but in the new structure unfortunately there's just no place for you."

"Oh. I… what is it, an overlapping of skills, is there someone at Çalış & Çalış who does what I do who's cheaper?"

"I can see why you'd think that, but no. No, we just can't see the value in what you do, to be honest. We're running the numbers in the lead up to this merger – which you can't fucking tell anyone about, by the way, and remember that you're still under contract – and we just don't see the business sense in continuing to employ you."

Who would I tell? "OK, but…"

"It's the nature of the word, 'redundant' – something that *isn't required*. Now, the HR handbook tells me that I should be telling you that we don't make people redundant, it's the *role* that gets made redundant. You know, to stop people killing themselves. But I reckon that's even more insulting, don't you? If I come in here and say *'Hey, mate, you know that thing you've been doing for the last twelve years? It turns out it's completely pointless and we've never needed it'*. Harsh, isn't it? So that's not what I'm telling you, although if HR ask then that's the official line I went with, right? No, after all this time I reckon you've earned a little honesty, so I'm just laying it on the line for you. We just don't need you. I'm sorry, but that's the way it is."

It's a little tricky to process, I'll admit. And I can't stop looking at his tie, it appears to have mustard on it. How do you get mustard on a tie? What does one eat at breakfast time that even involves mustard? "So, I mean… *fuck*."

"I'll remind you that this is an official meeting mate, keep the language in check."

"Sorry, I just… so what happens now? Is there a package? Do I work out my notice?"

"Nah mate, if you want you can pretty much just fuck off home now if you want to. I would. I got Finance to crunch the numbers for you, here's what we're offering."

He slips me a piece of paper. Payment in lieu for the official twelve weeks' notice, plus statutory redundancy, plus reimbursement for unused holiday time. About thirteen grand all-in.

"So I just… go?"

"Yes mate, I would. No point hanging around, is there?" He's checking his watch in that way self-important people love to do when they want you to know they have better places to be, and I can see that this whole conversation is an inconvenience in his busy day and I almost feel apologetic for taking up his time, in amongst the strong desire to grab him by the back of the head with both hands and force his face into the conference table over and over and over until it's nothing but a mashed and filthy collage of pulpy flesh and fragments of splintered bone, the cunt, but that's the old me and there's no sense in raising your blood pressure unduly over such things and I should probably just let him get on with his day, he's a busy man.

"What about my season ticket loan, does that get refunded?"

"I dunno mate, talk to HR. Listen, I've got to go to this thing so… we good, yeah? You're cool? Yes? *Yes?*"

"Yes, fine."

"Sweet, well take care."

And he's already on the phone to his secretary before he reaches the lifts, asking her to book somewhere for lunch, somewhere nice, and no it'll just be the two of them and she can order whatever she likes, and he knows he's a great boss but he loves to hear it sweetheart, she's a treasure.

The pub across the road is an anthropologically interesting place at eleven in the morning. You've got your perky but disheveled bar staff, alcohol still coursing through their veins from last night's shift and the double-espressos just starting to kick in, and you just know they pronounce it 'expresso'. You've got your harried execs, polishing off their plates of bacon and eggs as a cunning ruse to disguise the fact that they've also ordered a Fosters as a gassy pre-conference-call eye-opener. There's the stubbly old man in the motheaten cardigan sitting in the corner who's honestly such a cliché that I wouldn't be surprised if the management had ordered him from a catalogue sent over by head office along with the vomitously lurid carpet and the whimsical beermats with sub-Christmas cracker jokes on them. And of course there's the hollowed-out human carcasses who've just been made unexpectedly redundant after twelve fucking years of loyal service and decent appraisal performance and general sense of being a useful if not popular cog in the machine, although glancing around the room it's becoming increasingly obvious that I'm actually the only person who fits into the latter category. In the Venn diagram of early morning pub patrons, I do intersect strongly with the Fosters-drinking exec, but naturally I still have standards even in despair and I've gone for the guest ale thank you very much, which is a nice chewy thing from east Kent that presents such robustness of the palate that it might as well have twigs floating in it.

Twelve years. I'm not totally sure what to do with myself now, I'll be honest, and this has thrown my entire routine out of whack. What time is it? 11:10. This is generally the time that I eat my apple and think about making another cup of tea. I shouldn't be having a pint at this hour of the day. But I guess all of my shoulds and shouldn'ts have to be reassessed now, so sod it, I order another pint from the guy behind the bar who really looks like he should be called Brad or Chip or something equally 90210, god his hair's perfect, why are his teeth so white, and I gulp half of it back as soon as he passes it to me before settling back into the chair which has the weirdly curved arms my nan's old dining chairs used to have and is just sticky enough to be slightly unpleasant.

The big screen is tuned to BBC News 24, and isn't it interesting that we still say 'tuned' as if there's a knob on the front of the TV set that you have to twiddle, I remember when I was a kid we had a TV with four channels and when they launched Channel 5 we had to tune Channel 4 out and then remember to tune it back again, until we realised that Channel 5 didn't have anything worthwhile to offer and we stopped bothering. Televisions always had wood-effect casings too, what happened to that? The screen is showing helicopter footage of Waterloo Bridge, which seems odd given that it's not exactly a live crime scene now and they can't have much to gain from filming live. Helicopters must be expensive to charter too, mustn't they? Perhaps they just have it flying around all day anyway, and need to squeeze their value out somewhere. The angle it's hovering at would have provided a perfect view of the gunman sailing over me and into the Thames, had it been there at the time. I try to picture his face but, if anything, this morning's events have made me picture everyone at the scene as Jed, and that's not entirely helpful. There's a deep indentation to the barrier, that wonderfully engineered barrier, in the approximate position that I'd been crouching in, in fact from this angle it almost looks as if the car had managed to break right through, and I'm interested to note the deep winestain on the pavement, like the cheek of the girl in my class at school who always got bullied for her birthmark and god I felt sorry for her, that awkwardness must be with her forever. I'll have a look at that bloodstain on my way to the station. It's huge.

"Er... mate?" It's the casually disjointed tone of someone who doesn't know your name and possibly should but doesn't altogether care. It's Colin from Finance. I've known him for twelve years, he's been here longer than me.

Not 'here', no – it's *'there'* now. I need to rework that in my brain too.

"Are you, er, alright? You look a bit pale, mate."

"Colin. Yes. Yes, I'm alright thank you. Perfectly alright."

"It's just I heard that, you know…"

"I just fancied a drink Colin, perfectly normal thing to do in this vibrant cosmopolitan metropolis of ours, so I'm given to understand. I see you had the same idea?"

"Ha, no, I wouldn't be drinking at this time of day! Um, not that there's anything wrong with, you know… er, no, the catering people ran out of nuts and we've got clients coming in, so…"

"Right, yes, very wise. Anyway, I must be getting back to the office, Colin. Time waits for no man, and all that."

"*Really*? You're going back to the *office*?"

I'm not wholly enamoured with the tone of this question or the look which accompanies it, although Colin's always been a nice enough chap so I'm sure there's no malice underlying it and it'd definitely be an act of paranoia to assume he'd actually been dispatched to follow me in here.

Then again, my mouth has suddenly filled with cotton wool and my head feels as heavy as a fencing mask full of rocks and I can't muster a cheery response, I just fucking can't, although I'm sure he, you know, oh, fuck it all.

I'm sufficiently composed to proffer a cheery wave to the receptionist, the one true human in the place, by the time I stride confidently back into the building a few moments later, and isn't it refreshing what a tonic the summer air can be? I stare intently at the alarm button in the lift as it carries me up to the fifth floor, something I'd always dreamed of pressing just to see what happened and jeez I'd really like to press it right now, but that would possibly bring loads of attention directly to me and frankly that's the last thing I want. I enjoy a luxurious slash in the fragrantly scented gents as I ponder my next move, but I can't really work out what that's supposed to be so I simply go to my desk and sit down. Thirteen new emails. Someone else's empty crisp bag. Mug absent. Something not quite right which takes me a good few minutes to identify before I figure out that some wag has craftily swapped the 'M' and 'N' letters on my keyboard.

"Does anyone have a carrier bag to spare?"

No response at all, not even an imperceptible shake of the head from a single one of them, although to be fair I know everyone's quite busy at the moment and I'm hardly asking an interesting question, and hopefully most of them didn't actually hear after all as the question is sense-checking itself in my head and it sounds ridiculously inane and the more it repeats the worse it is. Thankfully I have a carrier bag myself, I remember, I was carrying my lunch in it yesterday and it's now in my bottom drawer, so I retrieve it and place my potted peace lily inside, the one I'd taken a cutting of to grow the one in my kitchen that's now far more successful, then I shut my computer down and carry the lily to the lift, take it back down to the ground floor, resisting the urge to press any non-essential buttons, and walk through the revolving door for the last time ever, suppressing the further urge to pin down the nearest extravagantly-bearded hipster creative type and explain in excruciating detail just how unjust it all was, and suddenly I'm feeling rather parched and do you know what, I might just pop in with my lily and have another pint because I have nothing else to do.

London is full of eccentrics. It's one of the things I've always really liked about it. You can wear a monocle, or a silk jumpsuit printed with luminous dragons, or dye your hair half-green half-pink, and no-one will look at you twice. But I'll tell you a really good way to make everyone look at you as if you're completely insane: sit at the bar of a gradually filling Wetherspoons, drink a quadruple-whisky (which you've had to order as separate drinks and combine into one glass, because they're the rules), and explain to a lush and verdant pot plant in animated fashion just how hard it is to maintain positivity in the face of the overwhelming shitshow that is reality. But we're all allowed a lapse every now and then. I probably wasn't the oddest character in there. And I'm reasonably confident the plant and I are still friends. Our mood was relatively buoyant as we headed down Fleet Street, even though there was a chalkboard outside one of the pubs bearing the slogan *'Who ate all our pies? You did!'*, which isn't very kind, I know I'm a bit doughy these days but I don't think it's deserving of public ridicule, although if today's demonstrated anything with absolute clarity it's that the marketing industry more than has the capacity to be unkind, and the pub's probably just being whimsical, and you're a sensitive flower aren't you? No, not you, peace lily. You're remarkably robust, as long as you get a dribble of water every other day.

There's a house on the road from the station that I've often been tempted to knock on the door of, because there's always a puddle in the little porch thing by the front door, and I'm reasonably confident that I can diagnose the cause of it and fix the problem because my house is dimensionally very similar and about the same age, and I bet they've got the same boiler setup as me. The pressure builds up in my boiler over time until it all gets too much, and this is one of the reasons why I can really relate to it on a personal level, until fluid starts leaking out, which I'm less able to specifically relate to but I can certainly empathise. That little puddle by the front door means that the last shower you had was too much for the system, and the pipe behind the wall by the front door's had to do a little wee. All you need to do is drain down the immersion and it stops doing it. But how do you open that conversation with a stranger, once you've taken the plunge and rung the doorbell?
Fuck it, I'm going to do it anyway. Nothing else normal has happened today, my intentions are good, perhaps the universe will smile on this act of kindness.

Ding-dong. Classic doorbell. That's how you'd write down a doorbell noise in the *Beano.*

"Hello?"

A harassed-looking woman, mid-thirties I'd say, and the sound of excitable children somewhere within.

"Er, yes, hi. I wanted to talk to you about your puddle."

"My… puddle?" She eyeballs the peace lily suspiciously, as if trying to connect some dots that are refusing to work together.

"Yes, this one, this leak down here."

"OK… what about it? *Stop that Macy, or I'll take it off you again!*" (That last part wasn't for me.)

"I think I can fix it for you."

"Oh, right, well I don't think we need a plumber right now, thank you." She goes to close the door.

"Wait, no, I'm not a plumber, I just…" but the door's already closed and I can hear her telling someone that no, she doesn't know, some nutter going on about water leaks, how should I know, fuck it, now the fish fingers are burning.

The puddle is not dissimilar in shape to the bloodstain on the bridge, and I ponder this as I continue my walk home, trying not to think about the suspicious eyes that may or not be boring into me from an upstairs window as I amble away, honestly miss, I'm not a lunatic, I'm really not, it's just turning into a bit of a day. The shape of Mexico, a sort of outline of a lying-down figure with an upturned bit at the end, or maybe more like Italy. Or perhaps not like a country at all, just the shape of a body from which the life has stickily leached.

Wilson's waiting in his car outside my house, and should I be surprised by that? He offers a cheery wave and climbs out as I approach, and the wave is a lot friendlier than the extremely official nature of what's gone before so I'm immediately suspicious but maybe that's the whisky talking.

"Hello, officer. Fancy seeing you here. Would you like to come in?"

"Detective Chief Inspector. Yes, thank you, I would."

It takes several attempts to enter the burglar alarm code as the uncharacteristic daytime boozing has turned my fingers into fidgety cricket-like things, and I see Wilson observing this with interest and there's no point making up a story about it so I just go with refreshing honesty, which I imagine is the sort of thing he'd enjoy. "I've had a few drinks, Detective Chief Inspector. I wouldn't usually, but it's been a bit of an unusual day."

"Brian, please. And yes, I expect if I'd been the subject of a terror attack I'd probably need the odd snifter to calm the nerves too, don't worry about it."

Ah yes, that.

"Well, actually, it's more… no, forget it, just a bad day at work." Might as well enjoy that phrase while I can, who knows when it might be relevant again. "Do you fancy a cuppa, Brian?"

"That'd be great, thanks. Milk and one, please."

I remember. I also remember that I didn't remember last time, and I bet he remembers too because remembering things is his bread-and-butter. I direct him toward the living room after I've flicked the kettle on, because I don't want chatting around the kitchen table to become our thing, that was mine and mum's thing, and I sink into my artfully grooved bum recess in the sofa as he perches on the armchair. Mum's armchair. But I'm sure she wouldn't mind, because he seems to know her so I'm confident that it's OK.

I catch him glancing at the urn a couple of times as his eyes scan the room, and honestly I'm starting to feel a little bit tired and I'm not all that keen for the conversation to be longer than it needs to be so I eliminate the inevitable pause by just blurting out "Yep, that's her. You knew her, then?"

He seems somewhat taken aback by the forthrightness, but I assume also relieved to eliminate the fluff, as you must get a lot of fluff in his line of work and he probably enjoys the efficiency of people getting right to the point.

"Er, yes, that's right. I knew Viv a little, years ago. We met at the hospital."

"Oh yes? You were a patient?" Was she your Androcles, taking the thorn from your paw?

"Well, yes and no. I was there on official business, as we had to arrest someone in A&E. He'd broken into a shed on an allotment, and as he was coming through the window he'd slipped and landed posterior-first on the handle of a rake, which…"

"No!"

"Yes, it was right up there. And a number of people had seen him staggering toward the hospital with this mighty protuberance poking out of his, er, rear end, and the trail of blood led back to the allotment where the break-in had been reported, so it was hardly Sherlock Holmes stuff. Thing was, the owner of the shed had found quite a lot of heroin scattered about in there, which doesn't just appear out of nowhere, you'd need to grow an awful lot of poppies, so we had a few questions to ask the fella."

"Of course."

"But unfortunately he got startled when he saw my colleague approaching and tried to make a run for it. Which, for obvious reasons, he was ill-equipped to do."

"Aha."

"And I was approaching from behind, so as he spun around I ended up receiving the clawed end of the rake right in the sort of place where you really don't want to be receiving the clawed end of a rake."

"Crikey. And mum helped to, um…"

"…to patch things up, yes."

Well, that's just the sort of thing I should have expected to be hearing today. Remember your dead mum? Yeah, here's a story about how she once manhandled my junk. Terrific.

The kettle clicks, and I get up and walk back through to the kitchen, desperately trying not to think about the severity of the mutilation to this near-strangers genitals as I rifle through the cupboards and find precisely no biscuits. But I gave him a meal last time, so hopefully the absence of dunkables today won't be chalked up as poor hospitality. I put extra milk in his tea to compensate, although it's far too white now and it basically looks like hot water with milk, so I have to get another teabag out of the tin and let that steep for a bit, but I leave it too long as I'm gazing out at my empty parking space and the whole endeavour's turning into a pathetic dead loss so I stop trying to patch it up and instead just make him a fresh cuppa, for goodness sake. Just relax. Inhale the comforting smell of violets. Pull it together, come on.

"I noticed your car's not there," he says, surprising at least some of the crap out of me, thankfully not literally, that'd be awful, as I hadn't heard him come in and I know every squeak and creak of the floorboards in that hallway. Detective Chief Inspectors must have a lightness of touch and fleetness of foot, it undoubtedly helps them in their day-to-day work.

"Yes, it's um… well, I think it's been stolen," I say, handing him the tea, and god I hope it's an acceptable colour, it still looks far too anaemic for my liking but people want what they want and 'quite milky' is a badge he wears with pride and enthusiasm, he as good as said so last time.

"Stolen? My word, when? I trust you've reported it?"

"Well, er, no actually, it must have happened last night, and I only noticed it this morning but I was late leaving the house and I had three minutes to catch up on my walking time, I have these sort of time markers along the route you see, and Jed had said he'd wanted *"a word"* and I was very keen for the *"word"* to be had, although in retrospect I'd really rather it hadn't been had because..." and before I know it I'm pouring out the whole story to him and twelve years, I mean really, what the fuck, and I can't think of a time I've spoken to someone this candidly since mum died, and he's passing me a crisp and freshly-laundered handkerchief because of course he carries such a thing and I hadn't realised until I'd finished the story but I'm actually sobbing quite a lot and my goodness he looks uncomfortable. Dammit, we're sitting at the kitchen table now anyway. It's like fate wanted it this way.

We drink our tea in that thoughtful and considered silence that all chewy subjects require to dissipate their gravitas throughout the immediate vicinity. After a few minutes, the thick, cloying air feels almost breathable again.

"Righto," he says, having swigged the last of his tea from the chipped Sally Ferries mug, and isn't it nice to see someone actually finish every last drop of a cup of tea, most people leave half-a-millimetre in the bottom as if it's some sort of courtesy. "Let's start by sorting out this car situation."

And already the dynamic in the room has shifted. The comforting hand on the shoulder has seamlessly slipped back to the official position, and is now reaching for the official notebook with its, I guess, official biro and its necessary brio.

"So you own the car, I take it?"

"Yes. I mean, it was my mum's, and she only had it because it was my dad's but he, er, and, you know, and so I didn't really even need it and I almost never drove it but it was mine and it was hers and..."

"It's alright, take it easy. Let's just take it one step at a time. It's a Vauxhall Cavalier, isn't it?"

"That's right."

"Yes, it's unusual to see them these days, I thought it was an interesting choice. A connoisseur's choice, you might say."

"Is it? I thought it was just a scabby old Vauxhall."

"Aye, to some people perhaps, but these are rare things these days."

"They are?"

"Of course. It's the sort of thing you used to see everywhere, but because they were so popular and ubiquitous no-one thought they were worth saving, so most of them ended up getting scrapped. It's like the old Mondeo in the nineties, do you remember those?"

"I… I guess."

"Same thing. No-one bothered to save them, so they just stopped existing. When's the last time you saw one?"

"I, um, I honestly have no idea, I don't really notice cars. They're like birds or grass, they're just, they're just there."

"Fair enough. But perhaps this context explains why your car may be desirable to some elements of society? Rarity means scarcity of parts, you see. There'll be a niche clique of people out there with Cavaliers who just can't find a replacement chrome bumper or a Rostyle wheel anywhere."

"I see."

"And if a sudden cache of parts arrives on eBay, they're not going to question where it came from. They'll just be glad of the opportunity."

"That makes sense. So you're saying someone's probably dismantling my car as we speak?"

"Well, let's not panic. Can you tell me the registration number?"

It takes some digging through the mess of old bills and bank statements and mortgage letters and pension updates, and oh hell, what's going to happen about my pension now, that was a work thing, do I just lose all that or will there be some way to get it back, I'll have to try to talk to HR if I haven't already been disavowed, and I find the car's registration document stuffed between a wodge of old payslips.

"DKG 494V."

"Thank you – and it's a brown 2000 GLS, isn't it?"

"Is it? I have no idea. Oh yes, it says here that it is. How did you remember that? Are you one of these car people?"

"You might say that I have a certain interest in the car, yes."

"You're not one of these bloodthirsty owners who'll be scouring eBay for my velour seats, are you?"

Evidently this is not the time for brevity, as he doesn't seem to like the insinuation. I was aiming for lighthearted, perhaps even borderline affectionate, although no, not like that, but I've clearly just struck out with downright offensive.

"I'll make sure the appropriate people are on the lookout immediately, sir," he says, all official again and maybe I shouldn't have dithered so much about the tea and perhaps the mood wouldn't have shifted so. "Right, I'd better be off," he goes on, exaggeratedly looking at his watch just like Jed had and I really wish he hadn't done that, it's the one thing I'll really be dwelling on after he's gone.

It's a good few minutes after he's driven away that it occurs to me he hadn't asked any questions at all about Waterloo Bridge, or provided any follow-up information about the driver, or... why was he here? Did he say? Perhaps if I hadn't been so revoltingly over-indulgent as to bang on about my day for so long then maybe he'd have had a chance to tell me, perhaps if I was listening to what was going on outside my head instead of being trapped so relentlessly inside it, but it's fine, we both enjoyed a nice cup of tea and that's probably the main thing and it's all alright.

I don't have the wherewithal to prepare a meal but there's a large bag of corn chips in the cupboard, and the thought occurs that if I tip them into a baking tray and grate a bunch of cheese over the top then it's something hot to eat and I can pretend it's a proper meal, plus it only takes a few minutes under the grill and thank Christ because the daytime hangover is one of nature's cruelest jokes and all of the morning ale and afternoon whisky has completely worn off now and sitting down just sounds like the best thing ever.

"Don't judge me, we don't have any vegetables," I say to the urn as I flick the TV on and switch off my brain to the cavorting idiocy of whatever they seem to be doing on this island today. Some sort of self-imposed challenge to do something wet that involves a lot of squealing and shouting 'oh my days', whatever that means. The pseudo-nachos are crack-like in their addictiveness, they hardly last a few minutes.

'We'. I mean I don't have any vegetables.

I place the tray to one side and fetch the urn, positioning it in its usual spot. Crook of the elbow. Not quite a cuddle, just... there.

Comfortably there.

There must be some scientific reason for its warmth. It doesn't sit in direct sunlight so that's not it, although now I think about it, it only seems to warm up when I'm sitting here with it, but hey, I'm not a scientist, there's a lot I don't understand and will never understand about the world, it doesn't pay to overthink these things, sometimes we need to just let things be.

Chapter Seven

Drip.

Drip.

Drip.

It doesn't bother me at all. Some people say that an incessant dripping is akin to a form of torture, that the unpredictability of what may or may not be patterns is more than the organised nature of the human brain is able to cope with, but I don't see it like that. I think it rather neatly mirrors the absurdity of the cosmos, the deliciously thrilling reality that it's impossible to predict what's coming next in life.

I say 'impossible'; there are large parts of my day that prove irritatingly easy to predict. Look at what's happening right now. I can see from the church clock across the square that it's precisely 11:10am… wait for it… *now* – and here I am standing in the same place as I was at 11:10 yesterday, and the day before, and the day before that, and the likelihood is that I'll be in precisely this spot tomorrow. The side entrance to the morgue, an anonymous and reassuringly sturdy oak door that serves as a sort of natural visual separation between the place where the bodies go and the lovely little bakery next door. Not that they're so lovely to me when I go in there though, although I never do any more, no point, they know I work in the morgue and they find my presence near their foodstuffs revolting. I don't blame them. I must come into contact with all sorts. But there's only so much water available and we can't all keep our hands clean at all times, the pathologists get priority because they're the top boys here, that goes without saying. I remember when pathology wasn't even a thing, but now this sort of place revolves around them, it's hard to remember what it was like when bodies were brought in and they weren't immediately dissected to have their tissues analysed under microscopes. I don't know what that involves and I couldn't confidently tell you what the point is but I listen, I listen, and I know these men are the ones who get listened to.

Leclerc, he's the chief, the pathologist among pathologists, they all bend to his will, the doctors, the police, the insurance men, everyone. He studied under the great Sarnois, and what he doesn't know about slicing bits off corpses and having a really good look at them probably isn't worth knowing.

I bent Leclerc's ear once about the growing nature of the morgue, I'd noticed a great many more bodies coming in in recent times, and it seems to me that expansion requires experienced and observant people to fill what newly-required roles may appear. I asked him about what steps I could take to becoming a morgue technician, if I could be the guy who assisted the medical examiners in preparing the bodies for autopsies, who cleaned and maintained the apparatus, who catalogued the effects of the deceased, but he was very keen to tell me that my niche was vital, that janitorial duties were indispensable, that I'd been here long enough to know every nook and cranny and, *mon dieu*, you don't just learn these things overnight and my long service had given me invaluable experience. And when the new morgue technician arrived shortly afterwards, with his *lycée professionnel* education and all his own teeth, I bore him no ill will.

So here I am at 11:10 every day, leaning on my broom, savouring the abrasive swell of a lungful of Gitanes, staring at the cracked face of the church clock and considering the nature of a drip that's nowhere near a water pipe and happens all summer long, regardless of whether it's been raining. A niggling thought at the back of my mind tries to convince me that I'm seeing all this for the first time, that it's all brand new to me, and yet I know I've seen it a thousand times before. Don't I? Haven't I?

It hasn't rained for a fortnight.

Drip.

Drip.

Drip.

Le Tournesol is an amusingly inappropriate name for a bar like this, populated as it is by shadowy characters in shadowy corners. It is neither heartwarmingly sunny nor bedecked with seasonal blooms. It's the sort of place where you spit on the floor because people would be suspicious of you if you didn't. It smells of drains, and armpits, and farts, and stale beer, which is perhaps the ultimate combination of appetite-quelling aromas, and that's just as well because Benoit's cassoulet contains things you really oughtn't ask too many questions about. It's only because I work in the morgue that I can be reasonably confident he doesn't get his gristle and skin from there. But the vet doesn't drink in here. Neither do the infirmary porters. Best not to think about it.

"Ugh," I grunt in Benoit's general direction, as few actual words are spoken in *Le Tournesol*, and he responds by waiting just long enough to be slightly irritating before shuffling over through the fetid straw and pouring out his trademark generous measure of pastis, to which I add no water because, in spite of the fact that it tastes much nicer when you do and you're treated to that glorious chemical sideshow as the translucent amber blurs into an opaque cream like watery custard, I just don't trust Benoit's water. I suspect the jug's never been washed, and there are things floating in there that may share their roots with the cassoulet ingredients.

I'm mulling over the overhearings of the day, shuffling into order the facts, the comings and goings, the seeings and doings. If Leclerc wants to keep me pegged at a janitorial level then that's fine, I have no problem with that, it's completely alright, but that doesn't stop me building up my knowledge about morgue matters to keep my options open, does it? This isn't the only place in France to process the deceased.

Much of my day, then, is spent in the shadows, creating the appearance of being busy while also maintaining an informative and revealing proximity to Leclerc, and his partner pathologist Espier, along with Pierron of course, the new morgue technician. Espier is by far the least discreet; a stumpy rural villager who seems almost incongruous working in a respected medical capacity, he looks more like the sort of scrote you'd find in *Le Tournesol*, scrubbed up and roughly combed and shoved into a white coat. He certainly smells like he works with the dead. Although who am I to judge?

I swill the undiluted pastis around its slender glass. This is the gateway drink, the eye-opener before I appeal to Benoit's better nature and see if he'll avail me of the good stuff. It's farmer's pride, having the best *eau de vie* in the region, and every dirty-necked rustic in every village is convinced that his fire-water is the one against which all others should be judged. Some have been distilled with raspberries or blackberries, others may have a whole pear suspended inside the bottle, hanging in limbo in the thick, slightly greasy but always devastatingly clear fluid. Wormwood is rare, as it's so uncontrollable in its results. Benoit favours the apple, and since he gambled on his simpler life and sold the family farm, disgusting the generations that came before him by ploughing the proceeds into the bar, he's always maintained that he's a farmer at heart and his apple stock is what now characterises the town. Or at least, the unseemly underbelly of the town, the level where the dirty work is done. (It's very important, of course, never to point out to him that running a bar with a purely reprobate clientele is far from a simple life. He counters that he doesn't have to get up before dawn any more, and there's no arguing with that. But he does get quite cross. Perhaps it turns out that selling out centuries of your family's work has its spiritual drawbacks.)

"We shall have to prepare for her." That's what Leclerc had said today. It's unlike him to spout truisms – we always have to prepare – so it piqued my interest and I cocked an ear closer. "She's a dangerous one, I'm not touching her." Espier had evidently been briefed on who was coming in tomorrow, and the look on his face was enough to curdle milk. He was agitated, shifting his weight from one foot to another and scratching his neck for far longer than could be necessary.
"We do what we do, surely there's nothing out of the ordinary? A body is a body." Pierron's inexperience expressed with an indifferent shrug, immediately shot down by the increasingly agitated Leclerc.
"Foolish boy! There are things inside this one, things we do not understand. What carried her away was… it was not of this world. Not of *our* world, at least. We operate in a field of certainties, and there is too little known about… about what is in this woman. This wretched, dangerous woman."
"But what can we do, brother?" asked Espier. "We know enough that it is dangerous. Is any of it worth the risk?"
"It is our function to mitigate risk, to assess these things and prevent them in future. The risk is not the concern, as such. It is the *variables* of the risk."

"I'm not sure I follow."

"No, I wouldn't expect you to. Pierron, prepare the apparatus, and secure the front-of-house."

"Secure?"

"Yes, secure, you know. Put black sheets over the windows, keep those *connard* vultures away, with their prying eyes. People know she's coming here, I've heard them whispering. We want no distractions, no rumours. After she is delivered, we answer the door to no-one."

"Benoit?" I waggle the glass in his direction. Speaking his name aloud indicates what I'm after, as that's really not the done thing except in particular circumstances, and he's in beneficial mood as he reaches under the bar to retrieve the unlabeled bottle of *eau de vie*. The measures are less generous than with the pastis, as there's love in this fluid and love means time, but you really don't need a lot of it to do the trick. It scythes down your throat like a thousand rusted sickles, it swims in your blood in seconds, annihilates the frontal lobes without mercy.

"*Hein*, Benoit, what do you know of this Curie?"

A shrug. A grunt.

"You know, this one from the sanatorium, up in the mountains."

"What the fuck would I know about that?"

"Come on *mec*, everyone's talking about it. And you talk to everyone."

Benoit picks his nose contemptuously, and sidles to the end of the bar to retrieve a glass, then joins me at the front and takes the stool next to me. He pours an eye-watering measure of the *eau de vie,* its oily haze distorting the air around the rim of the glass. He's silent for a long time, a good few minutes. Then he knocks the deathly apple back in one. "They say she's got the devil in her. Hostile spirits. There is much that is unexplained."

"No, surely not. She's respected, a scientist. Her work has helped countless people, it's advanced the field of understanding so much, so far."

"Why fucking ask, if this is what you think?" He pours a second, more restrained measure, and again throws it down in a single shot. I wince involuntarily, and he grins at my discomfort, trickling a meagre but potent top-up into the glass that's slightly shaking in my hand.

"The men, they're concerned," I say. "They're talking about

preparing for her arrival, but nobody knows how to prepare."

"Radium."

"Huh?"

"Radium, *putain*. It's the unknown quantity. You see, we live in a world of constants. If it rains, we get wet. The sun comes out, we dry. You touch mud, you get muddy. You walk in sand, you get sandy. One sits in paint, one ruins one's trousers. These are things we know."

I nod.

"But these things she discovered, she worked with, she ate and drank with and slept with and carried around, these are not like things we know. It is like witchcraft."

"Benoit, you are surely not saying…"

"Of course I'm fucking not, *connard*. I'm saying it's *like* witchcraft. You touch these things, and they don't make you dirty or sandy or wet. They don't seem to have any effect at all. But they get *inside* you, like demons. And these demons, they took her over and they finished her."

"And you think they lurk in the body after death, these demons, and wait for fresh victims?"

"Ah, but that is for you to find out. Let us see what state you're in when you come here and speak my name tomorrow."

Well, I've never seen anything like it. You could screen this at the flicks as a double-feature with a Chaplin movie. Pierron has fashioned himself a sort of airtight bathing suit combined with some manner of diver's helmet, it's completely absurd, I'm amazed he can see anything through that tiny window of glass as it steams up with every breath. It's all Leclerc can do to maintain a veneer of professionalism as Espier can't help flinching at every touch, as if the body may actually explode.

I observe with great interest. It surprises me that Leclerc is able to make incisions with any degree of accuracy considering the vast and cumbersome nature of the gloves he's selected – these are, it's safe to say, not the standard gloves you find in this room – but perhaps the weight of knowledge is pressing the blade down and guiding it true. The knowledge that the world awaits outside. The people, the press, the scientists, the politicians. What is in that brain? And that body? And why is it these gentlemen, with their social climbing barely masking their shitkicking rural roots, with their comical paucity of scientific knowledge and their fear of demons, should be the ones to analyse the results? Pierron runs from the room at the sight of the dark blood gently trickling from the first incision, the sound of him copiously vomiting – presumably having just got his ludicrous helmet off in time – offering a sobering counterpoint to the creamy-rich silence. Honestly, you'd think she was going to burst in a kaleidoscope of luminous green.

"And so he returns," says Benoit, from the far end of the bar. A measure of pastis waits in the usual spot.
"Indeed."
"And what did you learn?"
"Well, we didn't see any demons flying out, if that's what you mean."
He slams his fist down on the bar. "*Putain*! We know these demons, they are invisible, they enter you without you knowing, they eat you from inside, we know this!"
"We don't know this, it's merely speculation…"
"*Mais non*! You, you shut the fuck up, you get out!"
"What?"
"You heard me, get out! You're not welcome here, you and your demons!"
"*My* demons?"
"You know damn well, you were there, they've got you too. Everyone in that room, that cursed room, she's taken them all down with her. You want to infect the whole town? Tainted son of a bitch, you get the hell out of here and you don't come back."
I drain the pastis and sit for a moment, considering the bottles behind the bar which are never reached for. The essential tavern decoration that patrons of *Le Tournesol* wouldn't possibly consider an option; the Noilly Prat, the orgeat, the Chartreuse, the grenadine. So important to those who make them, so enjoyed by their admirers, but entirely out of context here and consequently of no value whatsoever. Context is everything. I throw a handful of centimes on the bar and, for the last time, walk out into the square.

Chapter Eight

Muffled thumps. Fervent mutterings. There's a taste of aniseed in my mouth as I awaken to the muted but insistent sounds of commotion. The lid is off the urn, and this provides a momentary horror, but nothing has spilled and everything that should be inside still appears to be so and my god, imagine if she'd got out, I can't even think how I'd separate her from the dust in the carpet to get her back in there. My days of picking things out of carpets are way behind me.

I place mum gently back on the mantel, lid tightly screwed on, commanding the room as she should, something made all the more obvious by the decoration of the urn which is a lurid scarlet with green palm leaves and aren't these things usually grey or something? And I absent-mindedly crumple the yellowing Gitanes packet into the wastepaper basket as I stumble down the hall to see what's happening. The familiar shadowiness has returned to the kitchen and just for a moment this provides an enormous sense of comfort as I allow myself to believe for a half-second that some benevolent soul has returned the car, but winding up the roller blind reveals the instantly crushing reality that it's just someone else's car which appears to have been parked on my driveway for some reason. But that's fine, it's not crushing, that's an overreaction; given that my car's no longer there it's not as if the drive was in use and perhaps it's a friend of a neighbour or something and I'm sure they'll be gone soon and it really doesn't matter, there are more important things to worry about. I mean, I always used to park nose-on as it seemed a healthier thing to do, as backing in as this person has means that the exhaust is pointing right at my kitchen window ready to billow carbon monoxide or whatever all over my corn flakes, but again there are bigger concerns in the world and I won't dwell on this, it's not healthy to dwell.

Rolling up the blind seems to trigger a sort of mayhem outside, as it turns out there are rather a lot of people out there and they're suddenly all focusing their eyes and their camera lenses on my window and… that's a bit weird isn't it? I don't remember winning the lottery, and I'm pretty sure I haven't killed anyone or had a famous actress over to stay, so I can't imagine why there's a *Notting Hill*-style crush of what seems to be reporters outside, but they've seen me now and evidently I am what they've come to see so I open the front door and offer a cheery good morning to all.

…and now they're all talking at once, which really does make it hard to separate one voice from another and it's impossible to answer any one individual when there's so much collective verbal chaos so I hold my hands aloft in an effort to quell the noise for a moment and implement some manner of reason and rationality, and it's only when it's a moment too late that I realise my hands had been holding my dressing gown closed in the breeze and as a gust of wind carries it wide open it becomes immediately apparent that I'm not wearing anything underneath and *fuck it all* why do these things happen *for fuck's sake*? I've just treated what I can only assume is half of Fleet Street to an inadvertent kinky peep show and there really were quite a lot of flashbulbs popping and my phone's beeping as I slam the front door shut and Jesus Christ that was an unfortunate gust of wind. But they came here to see me specifically for some reason and that reason is not because I'm a noted flasher and presumably they'll understand that it was just the horribly malicious weather and I'm sure it'll all be fine.

I open up the text message as I hurriedly try to put a pair of boxers on, which is not the most tactile way to do things as these are really both jobs that are best tackled separately so that you may devote the appropriate care and attention to each as otherwise you'll end up with your boxers half-on and backwards while your phone's gone into the 'settings' menu. I unhitch the pants, put them on properly, sit down, and read the message. It's from Stuart, and god knows which one he is, he's one of the people from the office who's merged into the generic bearded mass of it-could-be-any-colleague, letting me know that Jed has tipped off the press that I was there on the bridge that day and helpfully given them my address. I'm sure Jed was just trying to be helpful and the press would appreciate context to thicken out their story, they have jobs to do too, and I make a few attempts to type out a reply to Stuart but I can't for the life of me think which one he is as they all just look like Jed in my head now, and how did he get my number and why do I have his, and I drop the phone on the counter and open the front door again.

It's the same din, the mass of shouting, but the atmosphere seems a little more charged now. Unsurprisingly. I open and close my mouth like a fish a few times as my brain struggles to think of an

appropriate opener, stupid brain, but the guppy impression
seems to have the potential to further mark me out as a nutter so
I just opt to say anything and my brain decides to make me say
"I'm sorry about my cock".

Terrific.

At least they've quietened down. It's an edgy quiet, but it's
something.

"Um, what I mean to say is, er, sorry about that… that thing just
now, the wind, it was unfortunate, er…"

And suddenly they're all shouting again, and once more I raise
my hands for calm, this time in the thoroughly reassuring
knowledge that I have my boxers on and I've tied up the
dressing gown cord really tight just in case, like Arthur Dent,
and I say "OK, there's a lot of you asking questions at once but
most of them seem to be the same questions so I'll just… I don't
know, do I make a statement? Alright, so I was walking home
from work, and I was on the bridge, and you know what
happened, it was all over the news, well, you *are* the news so of
course you know, and the car was coming but then it wasn't
coming and then there was the gunman and he did lots of
shooting but then he was thrown in the river and there were a lot
of people and some of them were alright and some of them were
not alright and I'm sorry there's a lot of words in my head and
sometimes when they come out, the order, you know, and am I
going too fast and you seem to be having trouble making notes
of all this and I'm, I'm sorry, I should really, I don't know," and
is that the sound of a helicopter overhead or is it just the rushing
sound in my ears, and I'm on the driveway hugging my knees
and hiding my head and I can't, I can't stop weeping, and there's
just so many of them.

A lady, a kindly lady who smells faintly of violets, just like mum,
helps me to my feet and elbows reporters away left and right as
she helps me back to the door, and god she looks like my mother
when she was younger, her hair plastered to her forehead in the
driving rain, and I don't know what to say, but inside behind the
closed front door is immediately more comfortable and I just
switch it all off. Shut it out. Take stock of things: that's all out
there, but I'm in here, and here is my comfortable place. Breathe.
Calm. It is 9:10am. What do I normally do at this time of day?
Well, normally I wouldn't be here at this time on a weekday, but
'normal' has changed, context is everything, did someone say

that to me last night? Who could've, it was just me alone at home, was it not? So I make a cup of tea, because you know where you are with a cup of tea.

After half an hour or so, the car pulls off the driveway and the kitchen is bathed in light. Sweet, sarcastic sunlight. There's probably a fucking rainbow.

———————————————————

Drip.

Drip.

Drip.

It took me years to fathom how the roof leaked, it just doesn't make any sense. How can you be able hear the dripping of the rain onto the living room ceiling, when there's a bedroom above it and a loft above that? Surely it'd have to be dripping through the roof and down through the bedroom, and that'd be such a colossal and obvious leak that you'd presumably notice it and have to change a few things. It'd be like trying to sleep in a musty Atlantis. But no, when it first started happening it was a total mystery. I had a roofer round to redo the flashing, and then another one to do a better job because the first one was clearly a berk as it was still leaking, and someone to check all the window seals, and someone else who attempted to explain what soffits and facias were before it became obvious that literally no-one in the world knows or cares what those things are, and it was only when I bumped into Helen from next door while I was at the corner shop and we got chatting about this-and-that that she mentioned it happens in her house too, and the one on the other side. Apparently if the wind's blowing a certain way, it drives the rain up under the eaves and it drips into the cavity between the ground and first floors. Design flaw. A quirk. So that helped to quell the rage a bit. You know, in my rage days. So now, instead of storming about the place growing agitated and swearing at the stupid bastard motherfucking cocksucking prick of a roof, I can simply give it a wry smile and think of it as character. An idiosyncrasy. I'll just need to remember, on a sunnier day, to spray over the damp patch with a bit of gloss paint, then roller a splash of matt white over the top. It's fine.

Bloody hell, when did it all come to this? Ceilings. Paint. *Idiosyncrasies*. Flashing reporters. Alone. My teenage self would be drowning in despair.

Drip.

Drip.

[…]

[…]

Drip.

See, there was a time when that exaggerated pause between drips would have seemed sardonic, like a personal slight. As if the drips were deliberately teasing me, just to torture me, *you think we've stopped, but no, no, yes, have we, no… aha, we haven't.* But I just let these things wash over me now. No stress.
With my mug freshly charged with tea, I open up the laptop to see what the wider world may or may not be saying about what happened outside just now, because although I don't see myself as a particularly newsworthy entity there's clearly something the reporters want to report, and I'm aware that unexpected genital sideshows are just the kind of thing that social media really likes, and who knows, perhaps the news networks would enjoy a little comic relief to draw attention away from the bleakness of the tragedy. Am I happy to be the fall guy in this particular scenario? Well, if it brings a little light to the darkness then who am I to complain?
But the internet is not working. The router is flashing an angry red instead of its calm usual blue, and isn't that just a perfect visual representation of the morning so far? The really fun part is that the way to run diagnostics on the system and report faults is to use the tool on the provider's website, which obviously you cannot access if your internet is not working.
It is, however, well into the twenty-first century and the magic of smartphones is joyfully abundant, with all their delicious juicy

4G signal, and I'm sure the wifi will fix itself in due course, it usually does, nil desperandum, so I google myself on my phone instead, allowing myself a brief smile at the notion of 'googling myself on the toilet', a phrase my younger self would have been very much amused by.

Yep, there it is. Typing my name in reveals many, many results involving the words 'penis' and 'unfortunate', and that's not a life goal that features highly on anybody's list.

Hang on a minute... Gitanes? I don't even smoke, not these days. Where did...? Where can you even buy French fags around here? God, and I could do with a cheeky toke now though, that always made things a lot easier didn't it? If you're prone to being wound up, weed really is a marvellous way to chill the fuck out and shut the fuck up. Two things that have always figured highly in my aspirations. Crumbled up French cigs make excellent joints, they're so harsh, you feel like a misunderstood poet.

I remember it so clearly, my best buddy Chris and I sitting in my room, picking little black specks out of the carpet and trying to work out whether they were carelessly discarded bobbles of hash or just crumbled blobs of mud from our shoes. Licking a couple of little green Rizlas together, because buying the king-size ones was so obvious and if you were just buying a pack of greens and a pouch of Golden Virginia then you really didn't look that suspicious. Lay the conjoined paper out on the table. Sprinkle in a generous pinch of GV (or, if Chris's parents had been on a booze cruise lately, treat yourself to the baccy from a few dismembered Gauloises or Gitanes for that chic continental kick), then scatter in whatever meagre crumbs we'd pulled together from whatever was left of whenever it was we could last afford an eighth. Roll it tight, but not too tight, lick it to seal, but don't lick it too much, and rock-paper-scissors to decide who blazed it up. The sparks from the flint, the sizzle as the paper caught, the slight aroma of burning plastic as we realised that some of those things in the carpet definitely weren't discarded hash. And the warm feeling as whatever chemicals we'd found were allowed to permeate the system, course through the veins, the brain.

Funny how everything before the first toke is so clear. Nothing afterwards is. It's like the opposite of poitín.

Sometimes, feeling flush, we'd try to score skunk outside Brixton Tube station, which invariably turned out to be London's most expensive oregano. But we smoked it anyway, because a placebo high is pretty much the same thing. Kinda. If you're broke. And then dad caught us one day, I must have been sixteen, and he carefully and precisely stubbed the joint out in the crook of my elbow, right on the fat vein that runs across the centre, maintaining eye contact throughout, and explained that degenerate people do degenerate things, and reprobate teenagers grow up to be worthless sub-humans. So that was me told. And that joint, my last joint, stands as a totem, a clear divide, between the happy-go-lucky youth and the bitter, acerbic adult. The symbolism of it really was lost in the rage, which is a great shame as the misunderstood poet within any teenager would surely enjoy the artistic tension, the counterpoint between weed, which makes you mellow and relaxed, and my father, who didn't. In hindsight, it seems foolish to have given in and allowed myself to be consumed by rage, by anger, by negativity, rather than using him as some sort of springboard for growth. Particularly after he fucking left. When mum left me too, last year, I could see that with rather more clarity. So I said goodbye to my rage. Life is short, and it's certainly too short for that. Let the world do whatever the hell it wants, I shan't let it take me down. I was angry for too long. If I can survive dad, I can easily survive having my cock printed in the national newspapers, surely?

'Your life, ooh, it may be a dream...'
Mum's old Radiola still sounds as deliciously warm as it always did, and by the time I climb out from the little improvised nest beneath her bed it feels like high time I made some decisions. It's fair to say that my life's taken quite an unusual turn of late, or several turns in fact, so let's think about them one by one and see what's to be done, shall we?
First of all, the bridge.
Actually, no, let's come back to that. I'll make a cup of tea and give that the attention it deserves in due course. Secondly then, the redundancy.
Christ, and now there's nothing in the world I want more than just to flick the radio back on and climb back under that bed, but I'm already halfway down the stairs and I can see there's post on

the doormat along with a whole bunch of business cards, presumably from reporters, and who can resist picking up the post? It's one of those primal urges, someone's actually gone out of their way to send you a letter, it's tremendously exciting, even for a grown-up, and a grown-up is most assuredly what I am, and shit, it's just a phone bill and a gas bill and that's rubbish post, I shouldn't have bothered.

'Redundant'. It's a horrendous term, isn't it? 'We don't want you to work here any more, because we literally cannot see the point of you. We are going to pay you to go away.' Fucking hell. I mean, it's probably fine, I'm sure it's fine, one door closes and another one opens, I just have to keep an eye on all the metaphorical doors, whatever the hell they may be, and life will take care of itself. Surely.

I mean, twelve years, alright, but did I ever really want to be there anyway? Let me tell you about the principal things I learned working in that industry: people in advertising really love the sound of their own voices. They particularly love to talk about themselves. This makes sense, really – when you're in the business of crafting messages to illustrate how brilliant a product or service is, the language and the concept naturally bleeds through into your own speech patterns. It's Pavlovian. This is why there are so many meetings in advertising – so that your colleagues can fill you in on all the brilliant things they've achieved recently. I realised quite early on that out of the average one-hour meeting, there was about five minutes of useful information. So I just stopped going to them. A quick chat in the kitchen afterwards with someone who attended will tell you all you need to know. Then you've basically gained an extra fifty-five minutes with which to watch cat memes on YouTube. And phone calls? No good ever came of a phone call. Nothing's provable, there's no trail. And you'll inevitably find yourself lumbered at least once a day with some windy adland-old-guard gasbag who wants to bollock on about how wonderful things used to be and will be again if anyone ever sees the sense to implement this amazing idea he's had. It wears you down. The turning point for me came a few years ago when the agency decided to replace all the desk phones with headsets that plug into your computer. Aside from the obvious problem that there's no way to call IT if your computer breaks, it was also quite annoying to use, so I stopped answering the phone altogether.

And you know what? Nothing bad happened.

And you also learn not to expect anything at all to actually happen. It won't. People get sidetracked. There are always oodles of ideas flying about the place – new concepts for clients, fresh social strategies, planned trips to talks or exhibitions or shows, breakaway creative groups, after-hours social events, proprietary reports or studies or predictions… it's physically impossible to do it all. Again, out of every hour of chattering, there'll be about five minutes of realistically achievable ideas. At first, you're expecting all sorts of exciting things to occur and you take it personally when they don't. But it's fine, really. People aren't abandoning ideas to piss you off, they're just busy. Maybe I've already made my peace with redundancy. I mean, massive kick in the plums though it is, perhaps I shouldn't have been there in the first place.

But where am I now, exactly?

The clicking of the kettle switch snaps me into the necessity of thinking about the next thing. The big thing. The bridge. That was… that is… OK, the sanguine and serene new me finds ways to rationalise and justify things, that's just sensible, it's working really well for me. It's what mum would have wanted to see, a peaceful and happy me, and if I wasn't able to show her back then, then dammit I'll make amends now. But making peace with a terror attack? That's a stretch. I should go back there. I have to go back there. I have to go back there right now.

No, idiot, shut the door, go and have a shower and put some clothes on, then go back there. The world's seen quite enough of your ballbag today.

I can't help smiling at this. What a bloody silly-billy.

The small puddle is still sitting in the porch of the house near the station, and of course there's no reason why it shouldn't be, and it would probably be overjoyed to be joined by so many other sizeable puddles all over the drive, if puddles were capable of such emotional depth. There's a slight twitch of the curtain as I walk past at rain-speed (which is mildly swifter than am-I-going-to-miss-the-train speed; not quite a run, but enough of a clip to suppress the voice that likes to say *'Hey, this is a fair old walk, why don't you move closer to the station?'* every time it rains), and I wonder if she remembers me or if I was just a weird blip in her day, insignificant and thus safely filed under 'irrelevant'. To be fair, filing me under 'irrelevant' seems to be pretty common practice these days so I wouldn't blame her. But what if she knows I walk past here every day – or, er, walked, the tenses of my new reality haven't yet kicked in, it seems – and, more importantly, whether she's seen the images of my gust ambush. No, that's hideously vain, there's no reason why I'd even ping on her radar, relax. And this thought is comforting and warm, but my umbrella decides to blow inside-out at this point, leading me into that incredible split-second limbo when you think the umbrella might be saveable and once in a blue moon it is, but no, it explodes into a million slender metal rods and a sad fragment of flapping canvas, but that's fine as I'm thirty seconds from the station and it looks like the rain's easing off and I shouldn't get too wet on the way home later, hopefully.

The station platform, of course, doesn't have a canopy. Well, it does, but it's only small and it's jam-packed with moist commuters, so I have to stand in the rain. Which is no problem, as my train's due in two minutes' time.
But it is inevitably late, you could set your watch by the rail operator's shortcomings – y'know, if it was one of Salvador Dalí's watches – although seventeen minutes taking a shower in your clothes isn't the worst thing that could happen to a person. I've seen the worst thing that can happen to a person, really close up, so I'm sure I'll cope with being a bit damp for a bit, it's OK.

The bleak weather seems grimly appropriate to the scene on Waterloo Bridge, the tribute cards gently crumbling inside their poorly sealed cellophane sarcophagi, the banners artfully dissolving. The flowers look perky, at least. An art teacher might make some heavily stretched analogy about it representing a fusion of the beauty of rebirth and the inevitability of destruction, or something. Perhaps if I'd paid more attention to the world I could have formulated a convincing theory of my own along these lines, but instead I settle for leaning on the railings and gazing down into the murky brown-grey of the

Thames.

There are police sentries posted sporadically along both sides of the bridge, and the nearest one is eyeing me suspiciously (but perhaps he eyes everyone suspiciously, it's probably in the job description, I bet he's put it on his CV, 'strong interpersonal skills, acts on initiative, adept at eyeing people suspiciously') as I crouch down and read through the tribute cards, trying to match these names to the faces which my memory has already muddied and smudged until I can barely remember a distinct face at all. Céline Louvois. James Keyes. Barrie Abeyour. Floyd McRae. Carl Feaster. Harry Craganour. *'Forever in our hearts.'*

My mobile starts to ring, and as I stand up and attempt to retrieve it from my pocket, my sodden fingers slip and the phone shoots up into the air and arcs toward the water, ever so gracefully, just like that dead-eyed gunman, and bounces off the handrail. I leap forward, my foot slipping on the plastic wrapping of a bunch of flowers, and take the railing full in the ribs at high speed as, by some divine miracle, my outstretched hand manages to catch the phone before it plummets into the icy depths. I mean, really.

I crumple to the floor, the wind knocked out of me, and try to swipe to answer but my finger's too wet and the phone won't react, and the bounce from the railing has cracked the screen quite magnificently, and I scrabble to dry my thumb on the inside of my jacket and finally manage to answer the call.

"H…..h?" I manage, as that is all the breath I have in me.

"Ah yes, hello, it's Detective Chief Inspector Wilson here. Is this a good time?"

"Hnnnnnng," I heave, rather impressively I think, before having a good old cough just to really underscore the dramatic effect. "Hello?"

"Yes, I'm here. Sorry about that, I was…" [I pant for a bit, it's necessary] "…I mean, I'm just… what can I do for you, officer?"

"Detective Chief Inspector. I have some news for you about the investigation. It's, er, it's quite an unusual piece of news. Can we meet? Are you at home?"

"No, I'm on Waterl… I'm on my way home, I'll be there in about ninety minutes. You know, trains willing. Unusual how?"

"I think I'd better tell you in person."

"Oh go on, it'll niggle at me all the way home otherwise."

A lengthy, almost sarcastically long pause. "We've arrested Jed."

"Take a seat, officer. Do you mind if I just change into some dry clothes?"

"Of course, of course. And it's Detec… never mind. I'll put the kettle on while I wait, shall I?"

I nod in the affirmative, and squelch noisily upstairs, whispering an apology to mum about how I'm ruining the carpet, that was an expensive carpet, so expensive that she could only do the stairs and had to leave the bedrooms and the hallway for another day. That back burner fizzled out long ago. The stair carpet is probably the best thing in the house. Now look at it, all soggy.

When I reappear in the kitchen, crisp and dry like retro cooking oil, Wilson's at the table with a couple of steaming mugs in front of him, his grey herringbone suit perfectly dry, along with half a dozen Jammie Dodgers on a plate. This is an intriguing detail, as I don't recall ever buying any Jammie Dodgers, which means they must be his biscuits, and he's not carrying a bag or a briefcase or anything, which suggests that he must have had the biscuits in his pocket. Is this a normal way to behave? Perhaps it is, I really don't have a handle on 'normal' these days.

Jammie Dodgers have a reputation for being a kids' biscuit too, don't they? But perhaps that's unfair and requires reappraisal, like the KP Choc Dip. That snack, ideal Pot Noodle pudding, actually serves as the perfect Brexit metaphor, I couldn't help but notice – look at a Choc Dip pot, you'll see that it says *'biscuit sticks – 52%; dip – 48%'* on the side. Leavers are crunchy and firm, remainers are creamy and smooth. Jammie Dodgers are both, and thus presumably politically neutral. Like kids are. Yes, they are kids' biscuits. That's cleared that up. Wilson is a man who carries children's biscuits around with him.

"So… you've arrested Jed. My Jed? I mean, not *my* Jed, but my boss Jed?"

"Indeed, yes."

"Is this because of the images on the posters? Someone identified him from that?"

"Again, yes."

"Aha." Shit. I mean, maybe not shit, but… no, yes, shit, because it definitely wasn't him, he's a lot of things but he's not a terrorist. But maybe he is? Why would my brain make me describe him instead of what I saw; it sort of makes sense that he *is* what I actually saw? But no, it'd be a mad thing to do. What, he left work to jump in a knackered old car, pick up a heavily armed chum and go and try to mow down some pedestrians just down the road from his office? There's something about that which seems quite unlikely. But who says terrorists have to be rational? They have to come from somewhere, they have to have lives before their terrible acts, they don't just appear. Maybe it was him. But it can't be.

"Sir?"

Oh Christ, he's been talking for a while, hasn't he? "I'm sorry, I, er, zoned out for a minute there."

"I was saying, I understand that this must be an odd piece of news to digest. Particularly given the events of this morning."

"Events?"

"The, er… the pictures of you, you know, online…"

"Oh, please no, that was just a gust of wind, I'm not a flasher, I'm…"

"No, of course, we understand that. Could happen to anyone." He looks as if he really doesn't believe that's the case.

"Nevertheless, the arrest has caused some… difficulty."

"Difficulty?"

"Well, yes. Look at it from our point of view. You've just been made redundant, correct?"

"Yes."

"And when asked to describe the driver in this terror incident, you perfectly described the man who made you redundant."

"Ahh…"

"And naturally when he was pointed out by a member of the public – well, quite a few members of the public, in fact – we had no choice but to arrest him."

"Hmm."

"But you must see that there's a troubling connection. Not least that, if you'd seen him so clearly and knew that it was him, you could have just told us who he was."

"That… that is true."

"And he does appear to have a watertight alibi. At least, his rather effervescent PA was more than happy to vouch for his whereabouts. While also, I have to say, giving an unnecessarily enthusiastic appraisal of his character."

"Yes, I can imagine."

"So what I have to determine is whether you deliberately set us up to arrest this person you have a grievance with, thereby entirely wasting our time and resources and obstructing the investigation, or whether there was some other reason for describing him with such forensic clarity."

I sip my tea. I have entirely run out of words.

"I'll put you out of your misery, sir. I don't think you did it on purpose. I haven't come here to arrest you for perverting the course of justice."

That's a relief. Quite a big one. I inadvertently dribble a bit of tea out of the corner of my mouth as I raise my eyes to meet his steely gaze. No, it's not really steely at all, he has a friendly face. But, hold up… "Um, it's happened in the wrong order though," I stutter, with an annoying lack of suavity. Goddamn it, why can't I be 007 just once?

"I'm sorry?"

"I mean, you came round here with your photofit man *before* I got made redundant."

"Sketch artist. And yes, I had considered that, but we can't ignore the connection. And clearly there must have been some tension between you and him, regardless of when the, um, redundancy actually took place."

Hmm. "So you're saying…"

"I'm saying I think it's psychological. You described him because that was the only face you could picture. He troubles you."

No arguments there, I guess.

"You weren't trying to mislead us, but at the same time this stumble has slowed down the investigation considerably."

"So what does this mean, officer?"

"Detec… actually, Brian, please. Call me Brian."

"Of course, sorry officer. Er, Brian. So…"

"It means that I'm going to have to think about what we do next."

"I see." I don't.

"I had a phone call on the way here, Jed has already been released."

"Good, that's, that's good."

"Quite."

He finishes his tea, leisurely, a man completely at ease with the world and his place within it. I'm momentarily overswept by a colossal feeling of jealousy. But it passes, it's alright, we all walk this Earth to a different beat, or something. We can't all shimmer in doo-wop time.

"I'd better be going, then. I'll be in touch. And you know where I am if you need me."

"OK. Thank you, Officer Brian."

"And please make an effort to put some pants on before answering the door in future, if you can."

I have absolutely no idea whether or not this is a joke, and he's halfway down the street before I've managed to think up any sort of response, but sod it, he was really in command of that conversation and he can draw his own conclusions.

Shivering in the cool of the evening, I grab a beer – one from the cupboard, not the fridge, I can't face the fridge – and snuggle up with mum. The warmth is immediately soothing.

The reality show appears to have finished or been cancelled or something, but there's no need to panic as there's some sort of quite-similar programme about people competitively cooking cakes instead, the premise of which seems to be to spend a really long time baking a really posh cake which you then don't get to eat before a panel of judges arrive to taste it and tell you what's wrong with it, and that's exactly the sort of weird behaviour I need to allow my brain to switch off. Caramelised pears and sweet oblivion.

Chapter Nine

The sole of my foot has stopped itching now, which is a blessed relief as it had been troubling me for some time and I was starting to worry that it would lead to something more serious. I have no idea where the fishing net came from, but as I was stepping across the rocks a couple of weeks ago I stood on something which was very obviously not a rock, which extravagantly gashed my foot open and caused a rather festive amount of my precious lifeblood to dilute itself among the seawater. There weren't even any bloody fish in the net. And do you know how much it stings to bathe a fresh wound in salt water? Brings a tear to the eye, I can tell you. It must have been a cheap one, flax or something, as the brine had hardened and sharpened it like a thousand tiny knives.

It was typical of that day, of course. You don't expect to find a lot of decent-quality driftwood on even the best foraging mission, that's just a given, unless a ship's been dashed on The Points half a mile out and you're lucky enough to score some freshly tarred timber, but even so, there wasn't so much as a twig to be found. Decent wood is something I sorely need, as the rainwater's getting through the roof and there really isn't that much roof to begin with, so if it rains at night that means I'm not getting any sleep.

The fishing net was a bit of a turn-up, though. It's not the sort of thing I'd be able to make. Should come in handy for a bit of variety in the old diet. Rockpool crabs are a delicacy that I'm sure would go down a treat in the eateries of Whitstable, with that fancy new railway of theirs, or the Maine coast with all their clam beds and lobster grills, but if it's the core of your daily sustenance it can wear a bit bloody thin. Plus they're pinchy little bastards, I cannot fathom a cunning way to pick them up. And you can't just smash them with a rock, the shells disintegrate and mix in with the meat, making them basically inedible.

I ponder the deployment of the net as I see her walking along the cliff edge, the girl from Lyme Regis. I've never used such a net before, but how hard can it be? Presumably you just throw it in the water and it largely takes care of itself? As long as you tether it to something so it doesn't float away, it should be child's play. Free fish. Now, what can I tether it with?

She has a free and easy movement, that girl, scanning the ground with a relaxed eye, seeming to have a sense for what she's looking for and she's simply waiting for the opportunity whereby whatever it is she seeks presents itself to her.

Her presence has seen our community dwindle though, there's no denying that. In fact, I'm the only one left – the sole remaining forager on the shingles, as a parade of gawping onlookers arrive every day from Axminster and Yeovil and beyond. We even had a crowd from London last week, tippy-toeing along the shoreline as if they'd never seen the sea before, maybe they hadn't although I somehow doubt it, the gentlemen hoisting their silky trousers and the ladies immodestly hitching their shimmering skirts as they tittered and chortled and generally soured the atmos. *'Hey you, chappie,'* one of the fellows had shouted, *'have you seen her, the girl with the fossils?'*. Immediately recoiling as he came near, holding his nose as his womenfolk delicately gagged into their handkerchiefs. Shaking their heads in wonder as they walked away, *'Goodness, have they not heard of soap in Dorset?'* That's right, sod off back to the smoke, vultures. But I don't resent her, never could. Look at her, she's divine, sublime. Such grace as she shimmers down to the water's edge.

The others said she was ungodly, a heretic, her and her filthy ideas, claiming these things she found, these twisted rocks, were actually creatures, older than we could possibly imagine, making everything you read in the Bible an impossibility. Now, I'm open-minded, always have been, and I don't believe in shunning someone for having different ideas and opinions, but the others, oh, they hated her, hated her so much they left everything behind to start anew, escaped from the crowds and attention she invited to our little patch of coast. She brought the world to our door – well, not 'door', we don't have doors, not here – and they didn't like that, didn't want it, she shook the quietness out of our existence. The findings have been slim pickings too these days, there's no doubt about it. But I'm not leaving. Her presence makes the sunrise worthwhile. On the days that she's here, scouring like us but with a deeper purpose, we are one. Beautifully one. If only I could tell her. But I'm just a smelly shambles with a beard full of barnacles, I couldn't possibly approach her, could I? She's too... too perfect.

And there's that noise. Like... a lot of bells? But more, I don't know, like tin? I've never heard anything like it. It's a kind of a clang and a woo and a, hmm, I guess you'd describe it as a *beep* if you can imagine such a thing, and it's all happening at once, and god only knows where it's coming from.

There's a delicacy to the way the pebbles and rocks and sand shift as you sit on them, and it's probably my favourite thing in life. As the sun lowers itself toward the horizon, casting an endless orange torchlight across the dappled tops of the gentle waves and burning the day away, easing myself buttockward onto the beach and simply feeling the texture change is so gloriously divine. First the bigger flat rocks slide into their preferred position, then the pebbles and gravelly chunks beneath start to settle into a flatter plane, as if nature wants to create a perfect seat for you, desires your comfort, and then the sand at the base of it all compacts and absorbs what it needs to before shoring up a solid foundation for your backside. Those city types, they'll never understand the simple pleasure of feeling nature rearrange itself to accommodate your needs, working with you to help you relax. They're too caught up in their steam engines and pocket watches and opium and whatever else they feel they need to distract them from reality. This is the real stuff, right here. Me, and this pebbly beach, and this sunset. The gentle creaks from my shack as the breeze blows through its thin but dependable structure. The lapping of the waves, bringing bounty from the colonies or the Africas or all the other places in the world I'll never know anything about. Simplicity. You just need simplicity. Over-complicating life can only flood your brain.
"Mind if I sit with you?"
Oh my goodness, oh no, oh yes, it's her! What is… how… why is she still here, she's never here at sunset!
"Of course, please do, pleasure."
She lowers herself with impossible grace, and I just *melt* inside. Every fibre of my being instantly explained and rationalised and rendered redundant by her unrivalled magnificence. The ocean breeze holds its breath for a beat or two, in awed reverence at the wonder of her.
We gaze out over the water together, and I idly ponder whether there are any fish in the net.
"I'm Mary."
"Oh, I know. We all know, I mean, they, er, but yes…"
"We? It looks like just you here?"

"Yes. Yes, it is just me here. I am alone."

And we sit in silence, for that is all the sea requires of us.

It's not just the tourists that she brought, you see. Although god knows there were plenty of those, clamouring for trinkets and curios, things to act as conversation-starters in their silly houses and their silly cocktail parties, *'it's a dinosaur's toenail, you know, ha ha ha'*. It's the scientists. The men of learning. They have no respect for the beach, for the people who've made their lives there and resent the sudden arrival of a gaggle of entitled and bespectacled men, barking orders and putting up ropes and ordering teams of people around with shovels and trowels and strange little brushes and whatever else, setting up their tents like so many impromptu field hospitals and acting as if they own the bloody place. They were very excitable, the last lot, they said that she'd dug up a terror-saw, which sounds like a fairly unpleasant thing to me and I'm not sure I want to know any more about it, but dammit they'd all come from miles away to see it. Some of these things, they swam, and some of them, they flew, and every one of them is an affront to the Almighty, although presumably we don't need to believe in him any more if all of these creatures are proving that he was just made up for the sake of a book anyway. This is well beyond what someone like me should be thinking about. Food, shelter, not drowning in your sleep, that's the holy trinity for people like us. All of this new complexity is most unwelcome.

And so we watch the sun disappearing below the edge of the world, slowly but surely ticking another day off the celestial list. She's got a dog with her, and god I hate dogs, bloody yappy little things, but this one seems to be fairly docile. Little black-and-white scruff, happy to curl up alongside her and watch the sunset with us. I offer it a piece of crab, as that seems like the right thing to do, and it sniffs the morsel indifferently before turning its head away, and I really can't say I blame it.

Her breathing intrigues me, just ever-so-slightly louder than you might expect, and slightly shallow, which makes the lace around her sleeves and neckline shiver in deference to the gentle breeze, and I wonder how she keeps the hat in place while she's scouring the coastline, although I imagine there's some sort of arrangement of pins.

She spots me looking at her and turns to face me, intently, slightly questioningly it seems, and I'm not really sure how to respond to this as I spend so very much of my time appearing invisible to most people, and I can feel my cheeks starting to burn. But she doesn't seem to want anything from me beyond my quiet presence, and my god I'm glad she's sitting there. Even if she never says a word, this is a moment I'll cherish to the end of my days. Her, and the dying amber light.

She shifts the dog aside, and it appears it's been sitting on a little bag, a leather satchel affair with roses embroidered at the seams. She reaches inside and retrieves some manner of lumpy stone, and passes it to me. It's scratchy and solid, yet brittle at the extremes, and looks like a bundle of miniature cucumbers or a small pile of giblets.

"Scratch it," she says. "Rub it between your fingers. It has a truly peculiar texture."

Indeed it has, and I respond in the affirmative. "Where is it from?"

"Over there," she says, indicating off to the west, "beyond the head of that small cliff. I found it just yesterday, it's most intriguing."

"Is it? I mean, it is, but… why especially? I mean, what is it?"

"A bezoar stone."

I return a look of perfect blankness.

"A coprolite," she confirms.

Increased blankness, if such a thing is possible.

"Excrement. Fossilised dung."

"Aha." Suddenly I'm not so keen to stroke it.

"It's alright, it's not dung now. It *was* dung, millions of years ago, but it's had every single fibre of its being gradually replaced by mineral deposits. Silicates and calcium carbonates. It's at once a lump of dung, and a rock like any other. It exists in a sublime duality, it is both things at once. And isn't that a wonderful metaphor for reality?"

I nod, dumbly. I suppose if I had more schooling, or indeed any, I'd be in some sort of position to agree, or understand what a 'metter' was for. But I think I know what she's getting at. Life can be a piece of shit, but at the same time it really doesn't matter. I assume that's what she means. Although she'd never be so uncouth as to outline it in those terms, I'm sure.

She turns to face the ocean once more, and again we simply sit. Her, me, that dog, and her ancient shite. I cannot think of a more perfect evening. Is this love? It has to be love. I can feel her radiance swimming through every fibre of my own being; as the dinosaur crap was replaced with minerals, so my own flesh is being consumed by love.

And all the while those mysterious bells ring, louder, ever louder, near-deafening now, I can't believe I hadn't noticed how insistent they'd become, forcing their way through us, pushing out the freshly minted love in my body and smashing its replacement with a sheer cacophonous wall of noise, it's unbearable, I can't stand it…

Chapter Ten

Fucking burglar alarm. That *fucking* burglar alarm. Is there any more disgustingly jarring way to wake up, simultaneously flooding your brain with nausea at its hammering volume and awkwardness that it's early and everyone in the street is being awoken by the noise your house is making, and they'll all be groggily peeping through their curtains and cursing my name and *fuck it all* I'm tripping over my own feet as I stumble down the stairs and for a few heartbeats I can't remember what the code is and what the hell can it be and is it 4-2-9-1, that sounds right, no, wait, wasn't that the phone number in *One Foot in the Grave*, and in the mêlée I've dropped the coprolite and stood on it and gashed the sole of my foot open and oh, hang on, it's mum's birth year, must be, that was something easy for her to remember, and I punch in 1-9-4-9 and the house is suddenly as silent as the grave. Christ.

Since I'm up anyway I might as well put the kettle on, although as I flick the switch downward, three times since it keeps bouncing back up and turning itself off again, but that's fine it's probably just a weak spring and we all feel weak sometimes, I notice that the oven clock reads 05:22, and that really does feel like an extravagantly early time to be having a cup of tea. So I settle for a glass of water, and plonk myself down on the sofa to find a repeat of that thing about baking cakes from last night, as I must have dozed off and missed most of it. I can't remember anything about cakes, just something about… seafood? Dunno, but I can't remember what the bloody thing's called and typing 'cake' into the search box on the screen brings back a whole bunch of random results, although *Layer Cake* looks interesting as there's a screenshot of Daniel Craig holding a gun and I quite enjoyed him as Bond, so maybe this is the same kind of thing.

It is not the same kind of thing at all. You don't even get to learn the main character's name, and I hate that, it's a real slap in the face, how are you supposed to engage, but by the time the credits roll it's gone seven o'clock and it feels like entirely the right sort of time to have a cup of tea. So that, with gusto, is what I do. And then shower and shave and dress because goddamn it I want to feel normal, and how many other people from the office would have got up at half-five on a, oh, whatever day it is, to watch *Layer Cake*? This is deviating way too far from reality. So I'm out the door at 7:45, like a normal person might be, on the way to normal work in a normal way, and I might stop in at the café for a flat white because that is what normal people do, is it not?

The leaflets on the counter for muffin recipes and primary school jumble sales are looking decidedly dishevelled, as they've been shoved aside and splayed about in order to accommodate a bright purple and yellow box housing leaflets for a right-wing political party that I was sure had stopped existing, but evidently not, and I make a mental note to try to spill a little of my coffee on the purple ones when it arrives, just to restore the order and balance of decency and normality, and little acts of political rebellion are what everyone does these days, I've seen it on Twitter.

"Flat white," calls out the barista, thus making the fact that he'd asked for my name entirely redundant, and I wittily quip "Lovely, not a vanilla latte then," and he looks at me as if I'm the strangest thing he's ever seen and I realise that perhaps 8am comedy is not my forte so I simply thank him and leave the shop, immediately realising that I've forgotten to vandalise the purple leaflets and, oh well, the clanking chains of social media will have to grind another axe for the moment. Can you grind an axe with a chain? Probably not, but it isn't something I've ever tried, so who can say?

And oh, but isn't it a beautiful day? Look at the glorious sunlight dappling through the oak trees in the front gardens here, and how fabulously luxurious to have an oak tree in your garden, and I spin on my heel and head back into the café because I've suddenly realised that what would be really normal right now would be to have a bacon sandwich and once I've had the thought I can't think about anything else. The crackle, the sizzle, I'm sure they keep a bit of bacon on the go at all times to waft out the door and lure people in off the street, and it totally worked on me. The barista greets me as if he's never seen me before, which I'd have probably done in the same situation so fair play to him, and it's the work of a moment to whip up a bacon butty and charge me four quid for it, which really is an incredible amount of money for such a thing but frankly right now I'd have paid anything. Every molecule in my body yearns to be sitting on a park bench with a bacon sandwich and a coffee, watching the squirrels scamper up and down the trees, waving cheery hellos to passing dog-walkers, breathing in the crisp morning air, just *existing*.

And Jed is standing in the doorway of the shop as I go to leave, and what on earth is he doing here? He doesn't live anywhere near here, does he? So he can only realistically be here to see me, knowing I live around here, which is unsettling but perhaps he wants to try to make amends for the whole redundancy thing and *fucking up my life the fucking bastard* but there's no percentage in holding grudges is there, and I offer him one of the cheery hellos I'd been formulating for the dog-walkers, but apparently he's in no mood for pleasantries. The air seems to crackle around his sweatshirt-clad bicep, and funny, I'd never spotted it before, he's actually pretty beefy in certain areas, and as he retracts his clenched fist back level with his torso there's a flash of electricity in his eyes before he lunges at full animal pelt towards me, destruction in his soul, oblivion in his knuckles, and the punch connects with my lips, splitting the upper in lurid scarlet streams as my teeth puncture the skin between his knuckles, our blood mixing in horrific synthesis, and he pumps his fist mechanically into my face, over and over, my nose seemingly smooshing flat and feeling as if it's bursting like a tomato under a rubber mallet, and really now this isn't necessary at all. The barista, revealing himself to be unexpectedly handy, launches us both out and onto the pavement before I realise he's even moved from behind the counter, and I'm annoyed to note that I probably won't be welcomed back here again, although there are other coffee shops so I'm sure it won't be too much of an issue, it's more of a dignity thing than anything, and Jed and I lie side by side on the pavement, breathing heavily, the momentum gone. From the corner of my eye I can see that my bacon sandwich, still neatly sealed in its paper bag, is lying on the floor just inside the door; the coffee's gone, or rather it's everywhere, but the sandwich is saveable, so after staunching the extravagant flow of blood from my left nostril with a paper napkin – why only the left? – I tippy-toe to the door making shrugging excuse-me-sir-I'm-just-going-to-pick-this-up motions like you would if you'd gone to pick up your keys having found yourself uninvited at a sleepover or an orgy, scoop up the bag, and step away from the café for presumably the last time, as Jed's getting to his feet.

"Um… fancy going to the park?" I say. And he shrugs, seemingly awash with conflicting emotions, so we walk together to the end of the street, through the wrought iron gate, and perch on the bench a hundred yards up the path, in rather different mood than I'd initially been hoping for.

He's not saying anything, so I open up the bag and start eating the sandwich. There are no dog-walkers, which is a disappointment, although there is a squirrel nearby which at least provides part of the picture. I toss it a morsel of bread, but it just looks at me with the sort of contempt that people with mashed-up faces probably deserve. I don't blame him. It's a nice area, he's presumably used to being given chunks of multiseed bloomer or fresh brioche, I wouldn't settle for cheap café Mighty White in his position either.

Maybe he just wants an acorn. I don't have any of those.

I proffer the other half of the sandwich to Jed, as it seems like the right thing to do.

"Fuck off."

Fair enough. I work a finger down into my shoe and idly scratch the sole of my foot, noticing with interest just how much blood there is on said digit when I retrieve it, to match the blood colourfully splashed across my hoodie. Really shows up on the grey marl too, there's no styling that out.

"So… what are you doing here, Jed?"

He pauses. It's never been nice when he pauses, it's like a vacuum opens up and the entire universe teeters on the brink, deciding whether or not to keep existing or simply to tumble inside and stop everything forever. "You motherfucker," he says, at length, and it's probably about as wholesome an outburst as could be expected in the circumstances.

"You told them I was a terrorist," he goes on, and things are starting to get a little clearer.

"Oh, *that*. Um… yes, well, they asked me for a description, you know, of what I saw, they wanted to know what the driver looked like, and I described him as best I could, and I suppose perhaps he might have looked a little like you and those must have been some of the details they picked up on, and…"

"Bullshit. *Bullshit!*" He's pulling a piece of paper out of his pocket, and oh no, it's one of the posters, and Christ it really does look exactly like him. There's no ambiguity there. I can see why he'd be annoyed. "You fucking described me perfectly, you piece of shit! You told the police I was a terrorist, and then over thirty people gave the police my name after seeing these posters."

"Ah…"

"Over *thirty*! Some of them were from the fucking office. I know who they are though, traitors, they'll be gone by the end of the week, you see if they aren't, just like you. Except without the fucking payout. It's lucky I had such a watertight alibi or they'd be shipping me off to Guantánamo as we speak."

"Look, I am sorry about that, I really can't explain why…"

"I don't want you to fucking explain."

"You don't?"

He takes a knife from his boot, and bloody hell, he's wearing boots like Crocodile Dundee, that'd be hilarious if he hadn't just taken quite a large knife out of one of them. "No. I don't."

And thank goodness for the late arrival of the dog-walkers, they may have missed their initial cue but they're bang on time now, and as I leap from the bench and sprint off he's immediately entangled in the leads of three soppy-looking Dulux-style clusters of canine fuzz, and I can hear the knife clanging onto the ruptured and ageing tarmac of the path as I pad, impressively athletically I reckon, across the moist and mossy grass, and I really hope he didn't check the HR files for my address before he came to track me down, but I suppose he must have done, although if he doesn't know the area then he won't be aware that this alleyway cuts back along the bottom end of the gardens toward the river, and channelling my inner ten-year-old I grab a long branch and swing Tarzan-like across the stream to the dense nettle patch that separates the hidden green space from the garden fences, and I have no idea if those are his footsteps I hear running in the distance but I'm not going to waste the time to look. I clamber over my back fence and drop messily into the rosebushes at the end of the garden, which would normally have hurt quite a lot with all the prickly thorns and whatnot, but given how the morning's going it's really just another irritation, and I scamper up the side path and tumble in through the front door, deadbolting it, safe. The comforting smell of violets is like a warm, gentle embrace.

A number of neighbours have popped terse notes about the alarm through the letterbox, although frankly I'm experiencing quite a lot of alarm of my own right now as I vault the stairs and dive down under mum's bed, not to hide this time although I really can't think of anything I'd rather do, but instead to retrieve her old leatherette suitcase. Because a plan is starting to formulate, and there isn't a lot of time to enact it before the window of opportunity closes. I risk a peep through the curtains and shit, there he is, he's running up the street, must've come the regular long way round, and he's seen me and fuck me he looks furious, so I start to gather what I need because I really have run out of time here. Shit, what do I need? Passport, that's item one. Wallet, keys, phone, the holy trinity, anything beyond that is a bonus. Oh yeah, phone charger. Pants, socks. Toothbrush, deodorant. Do I have time to change into a less blood-saturated jumper? Nope, just throw a couple of hoodies in the case, that'll be fine. Is that everything? Almost, just one more thing…

The duct tape is in the stuff drawer in the kitchen, the drawer that overflows with the myriad it'll-be-useful-one-day things like fuses and shoelaces and paperclips and AAA batteries and all that crap, and I use the thick black tape to secure the lid firmly on the urn before enveloping it in a sleeve of handy bubble wrap that must have come from some Christmas gift or other, and that goes in the suitcase too. Jed's hammering on the front door, kicking and spitting, and I have no idea how much of that abuse the hinges can take, but he'll never expect me to leave out the back, surely, so I escape through the patio door and off the way I came, through the roses and over the fence, wading across the stream with the suitcase over my head, down the alley, into the nearest taxi and away.

"Where to, mate?"

"Go, fucking go, just drive, *drive*!"

"Alright chief, there's no need for the language. You know, I always say…"

"*Just drive the fucking car! GO!*"

And mercifully he does, which comes as a great relief because my plan to outfox Jed by sneaking out the back door clearly didn't stymie him for long and he's sprinting right up behind the cab as the driver eventually pulls away.

"Ahem. Sorry about that," I say, trying to create the impression of being calm and rational and just another normal passenger who isn't in the habit of screaming obscenities at taxi drivers. I'm keenly aware that I'm rather liberally coated in blood and, although the cab was passing through the shadows of those

wonderful oak trees as I dived in, it's making itself glaringly
evident to the cabbie as we trundle through the sunshine that he
appears to have taken some manner of psycho on board.

"Listen, this blood, it's my blood, I'm not a nutter."

"Er… OK, if you say so, guv'nor."

"Really, this all came out of my nose."

"Yeah. Yes, well, you do look a bit banged up, mate – but you
have to admit that the way you got into the cab was a bit…
urgent?"

"Well, yes, there is a nutter, that part's undeniable, but it's not
me. I'm being chased, you see."

"Chased?"

"Sure, like in a movie. I know, terribly exciting. So if you
wouldn't mind stepping on it a bit, that'd do a lot to help slow
my heartrate down a smidge."

"It's a thirty, mate."

"Huh?"

"It's a thirty mile-an-hour limit, this is all you're gonna get from
me here."

"Oh. OK, fair enough."

"Your mate doesn't seem to be behind us, if that's any help."
I hadn't been brave enough to look. "Good. Good. That's…"

"Look, d'you mind if I ask where we're going?"

"Ah, ha ha – sure, take me to a car rental place please."

"Oh, no problem. Place on the high street do you?"

"Um… can you take me to one in a different town? Take your
pick. I don't fancy filling out all the forms with the possibility
that he might appear through the door."

"He? Your mate back there?"

"Funnily enough, he's not my mate. But if you could…"

"Of course. Leatherhead it is."

"Perfect."

I suspect the taxi driver and I won't become firm and lifelong
friends, but he gives me the sort of look I assume doting fathers
must give as I massively over-tip him, and he does seem
genuinely pleased to have performed a service in harrying me
away from a lunatic with a knife, so at least I've infused his
morning with a delicious flavour of drama and the satisfaction of
a good deed done. And I'm very pleased that I had the presence
of mind to change into a clean jumper *en route*, as the suspicious

stare the chap behind the desk is giving me is probably peanuts compared to the lock-the-door-and-call-the-police routine that would have happened if I'd turned up looking like a pivotal character from *Scream*.

"Christ, you been in the wars, pal?"

I immediately like this guy. No messing about here.

"Yeah, bit of a morning. Listen, I need a car."

An amused smirk. "Och, you've come to the right place."

"OK, I…"

"We do have one or two o' those."

"Great, because…"

"We can even lend one to you if you…"

"Right, shut up a minute, I really fucking need a car right now, OK?"

Shit. That's soured the atmosphere. Just when it seemed like we might be about to start getting along.

"Look, I'm sorry, I'm just having kind of a terrible morning. As you can see, I've had a bit of an accident, and my car was stolen recently and the police haven't been able to find it, and it's just become apparent that I really need a car today, and the situation's come to a head rather quickly, and I'm a bit stressed out to be honest, and I'm really sorry for swearing just then, you seem like a lovely chap, I've always liked a Scottish accent, you always sound so friendly, even Begbie in *Trainspotting* sounded like a gent when he was glassing people, and can you please help me?"

He eyeballs me for a discomforting amount of time, enough for it to feel like well over a minute, but it could be only a few seconds, I'm losing perspective by the moment today, and then his face splits with a magnificent beaming smile and I genuinely might be in danger of hugging him. That happy face. Aren't people great? I've got a lot of time for humans, in the right context.

"No bother, pal. What kind of motor are ye after?"

"Oh, I don't know, just a car."

"We can offer you a Fiesta-or-similar, we've got shitloads of them."

"Fiesta-or-similar?"

"Aye, it means it might be a Fiesta, or it might be something else of the same size. It's a bit of a lottery. Makes life exciting, see?"

"I see. I think maybe something a bit bigger?"

"Sure, sure. How does an Insignia-or-similar sound?"

The way he says 'similar' is magnificent, it rattles around in my brain for a few moments, luxuriating in its own offbeat vowel sounds. *Suh-muh-luh. Suh-muh-luh.* "I don't know, what is it?"

"It's a Vauxhall. Medium-to largeish sort of thing, like you see reps dozing in in motorway service car parks with a crumpled shirt on a hanger in the back."

A Vauxhall. I know where I am with them. The amount of times we did this journey in the old Cavalier when I was a kid. That'll be just the job. "Perfect, I'll take that one."

"Well fuckin' *great*, because this is your lucky day, pal!"

"Is it?" It really doesn't feel that way.

"You, my brother, have just won the rental car *lottery*!"

"…?"

"I've got for you, my good man, a delivery-mileage 530d, fresh from the factory and ready for you to enjoy, *sir*."

"A five… a what?"

"It's a BMW."

"Oh. Good, they're good aren't they? So I don't get a Vauxhall?" He looks slightly deflated, like I should be gratefully accepting wonderful news but have instead just knocked his chips on the floor, although he quickly rallies and comes around the desk to put his hand on my shoulder.

"Come with me pal, and let's get you sorted out."

He encourages me toward the door, ripping off his name badge and flinging it behind the desk, which seems like an odd thing to do. "Don't we have to, er, fill out some paperwork or something first?" I ask.

"Nah, I'll take care of that pal, no bother. To be honest with ye, it's mah last fuckin' day today and I've pretty much checked out anyway. Gi' us a lift to the car park down the road and you can be on your way."

"Oh… thank you, that's really helpful. Is this it?" We're standing next to a huge dark blue car, way bigger than I could possibly need, and he blips the key, the orange flashes indicating that this is indeed the case. There's an amused tutorial as he explains to me that handbrakes are often electric and controlled by a button these days (honestly, what's wrong with having a handle, why overcomplicate things for goodness' sake, it's just one more thing to go wrong in the future), and you have to push a button to start the thing instead of turning the key, which seems to me like exactly the same level of effort to achieve the same end, and then we're off down the road and he's lighting a joint the size of a Sharpie and evidently having a very nice time. Some customers are entering the shop, and this makes him laugh quite a lot. "Be thankful you arrived when you did pal, because those fuckers ain't gettin' a car today!"

At the end of the street he signals for me to pull into a car park, and he tugs another BMW key from his pocket. "Fuckin' boss has an M5," he says. "Rude not to, eh?"

I have no idea what that means, but he seems keen to get on his way and I'm certainly keen to be on mine, I'm still half-convinced that Jed's going to improbably pop up at some point and he'd be *really* cross this time, so I point the nose of the pointlessly large land-barge toward the M25 and head off Dover-wards. There's a huge map on the dash and I have absolutely no idea how it works, but people have been navigating by road signs for generations and I'm more than capable of doing that. Just reading and following arrows, isn't it? Easy. It's what mum would do. In fact…

I pull into a layby, furtively peeping around for signs of mental bastards with knives – well, one mental bastard in particular, anyway – and liberate mum's urn from the suitcase, ripping off the bubble wrap and strapping the warm pot into the passenger seat so that we can road trip together. Something I never thought I'd do again. Perhaps this day's not working out too badly after all.

"I'd like a ferry ticket, please."

"Well, you've come to the right place."

Fucksake, not this again. Although it did work out alright last time so let's not be too quick to judge. All things considered, the day could be far worse, so engaging in this sort of merry badinage is probably quite healthy.

"Absolutely, yes. What I mean is, I want to get on the next available crossing. I can see there's a ferry over there. Can I get on that one?"

"Where… what, that big blue one?"

"Uh-huh."

"That's not a ferry sir, that's the new toilet block."

"Oh. It's… it's quite big, isn't it?"

"Indeed it is, and you'll be pleased to know that entrance to the latrines requires no ticket or admission fee whatsoever."

"Splendid. And the ferry ticket itself?"

"There's a boat departing for Calais in twenty minutes, sir, if that's where you're headed. Usually we'd require people to check in forty-five minutes before departure but, as I always say, life's too short to fuck about with small print and red tape."

"Oh! Well, quite. One ticket for that one then, please." I'm experiencing a renewed appreciation for the service industry today. Things seem to happen a lot more easily if people just stop caring quite so much. Perhaps there's a greater lesson for life itself here. Maybe these people have relinquished their anger too? I must be among kindred spirits.

"When are you coming back?"

"I'm not entirely sure. I might not be."

"No problem, a one-way ticket. Got a passport?"

I hand it over, glorious in its crimson compactness. I never did like the big old blue ones, way too much baggage attached. And they didn't fit in your pocket.

"What's your registration number?"

"I have no idea, it's not my car."

A quizzical eyebrow is raised

"I mean, it's a rental."

"Uh-huh. Did you agree with the rental firm that you'd be taking it abroad?"

"Nope."

"Ah well, fuck it eh? That'll be seventy-six pounds."

I hand over the exact money in cash, which he seems noticeably impressed by, and I can't help feel a tingle of pride at doing such a grown-up thing so nonchalantly. I wonder if I should tip him? No, that'd probably be weird.

"Sweet, hang this over your rear-view mirror, follow the signs, and you're golden. There's a speed limit of 20mph in the terminal, but I'd suggest putting your foot down a bit unless you want to leap over the water and crash onto the deck like the Dukes of Hazzard."

"Okey doke. Did the Dukes of Hazzard do a lot of jumping onto ferries?"

"I'd go if I were you, sir."

So I do, and brilliantly the line I'm signalled into is already driving onto the vehicle deck. It's starting to feel as if this plan is actually coming together.

"Here we go, mum," I say, as we bump up the suspiciously rusty metal ramp, calling back memories of the borderline-derelict old Townsend-Thoresen ferries that used to rattle us across the channel, which I immediately have to repress lest they conjure up waves of nausea. "Back to Sauveterre-de-Rouergue, at last." Which is a cheesy thing to say, as well as a somewhat redundant turn of phrase, but it does feel pleasantly theatrical to narrate this bit as it's the kind of thing she would have said, and now I'm torn as to whether I should leave her in the car or take her with me. Walking around a cross-channel ferry carrying an urn containing the ashes of your dead mother is the behaviour of a crazy person and I'm certainly not that, I'm sure of it, so it's definitely best to leave her in the car. But I can't just abandon her strapped into the passenger seat, that also looks mental, what if someone peers through the window and sees?

But sod it, I'll just throw my coat over her, it'll be fine. She won't mind.

OK then. To the bar!

The bar is where we'd always head to as soon as we got on the ferry, mum and dad and me. He'd go to rustle up some drinks and crisps while she'd shuffle a deck of cards, laying down a hand of rummy ready for his return. The first set would sometimes be a joke hand, in which case mum and I would carefully arrange the cards so that we both had a winning hand immediately, and that would piss dad off no end and he'd huff outside for a cigarette before deigning to come back inside and play with us. On the tray he brought would invariably be a pint of lager, a gin-and-slim, and a coke, along with a couple of packets of Nik-Naks – one Nice 'n' Spicy, one Scampi 'n' Lemon. Regular as clockwork, every single trip. It was the sustenance package which signalled that we were on our way.

I consider buying all of these things now, but it feels a bit like Alan Partridge ordering a ladyboy, so I instead settle for the two packets of Nik-Naks and a pint, but the barman tells me he's not sure whether Nik-Naks exist any more and they certainly don't sell them, and *fuck it all*, and I briefly consider just removing all the complexity from the day and running outside to strip off all my clothes and leap off the back of the boat, for goodness' sake, I mean *really*.

"We have Quavers," he says.

Fine. That's a pretty good option, actually. But I don't want to sit at a table alone, it's a massive room with nobody in it and the exposure of being the focal point in such a scenario is frankly more than I can bear, so I sit at the bar and sup my beer as the murky grey water swells past on the other side of the filthy window glass.

"I know a joke about Quavers," says the barman.

"Oh yes? Go on."

"Yeah, it's… what is it? Hang on, let me think a minute. OK, yeah: A man goes to the doctor, and he says 'Doctor, doctor, my dick's turned yellow.' And the doctor runs all these test on him, right, and it ain't jaundice, and there's nothing wrong with his liver, and all of that business, you know, and the doctor can't fathom it out at all."

"Uh-huh?"

"And the doc says to the geezer, 'Tell me about your lifestyle. What do you do with your days?' And this man, he says, 'Oh, not much,' he says, 'I usually just sit around the gaff watching porn and eating Quavers.'"

"Right."

"Um… that's it."

"Oh. Ha ha! Very good."

"Alright, I know it ain't…"

"To be honest, I think the fact that you told me it was about Quavers at the start sort of ruined the surprise."

"Fair dos, fair dos. You know a better one, then?"

I really don't think I do. I've always been terrible at remembering jokes. I drain my beer as I search through the creaking memory banks, and the barman refills my glass with a fresh pint without being asked, which seems like a beautifully classic way to behave, reading the clientele, reusing the glass, and all of a sudden something flashes back from across the swirling mists of time.

"Actually, I do have a joke."

"Go on, then."

"Did you hear the one about the mathematician who was scared of negative numbers?"

"Nope."

"He'd stop at nothing to avoid them."
"…"
"…"
"I… yer what?"
"OK, never mind. I've got another one. So, there's this woman who's nine months pregnant, and she's been getting nervous as the due date's getting closer, and one day she starts to feel these twinges. She tries to ignore them at first, because she knows all about the false starts and everything that she'd been told about in the prenatal classes, but after a while it's getting too much to bear and she says to her husband, 'I think it's time we went to the hospital.' So they drive down there, and she's really in a state by this point, the pain's unbearable, and the paramedics help to lift her out of the car and into a wheelchair and they wheel her into the hospital, and all the time she's yelling out 'Shouldn't! Can't! Wouldn't! Don't! Couldn't!' And the husband's beside himself too, he's saying to the paramedics 'Why's she saying that, is she in danger? She sounds terrified.' And they say 'Oh, don't worry sir, they're just contractions.'"
An uncomfortable silence.
"So anyway, that'll be nine pound forty, please," says the barman, at length.
I throw a tenner onto the bar. "Cheers, mate. I'd better go and check out the duty free anyway."
It'll percolate with him, I'm sure. He'll probably burst out laughing in half an hour when he gets it.

There's a fabulous unpleasantness to standing at the back of the boat and looking down at the churning waters as they pass beneath you, the wake of the ferry bubbling the sea into the sort of spittle you find flecking the chin of an elderly and half-forgotten relative in some dank and dimly-lit home. Hollywood conditions us to believe that the oceans are beautiful and aspirational things, crystal-clear and more blue than your child-like whimsy can possibly imagine, but the English Channel is none of these things. It is grey and dismal and radiates an aura of basically being a watery manifestation of the concept of despair. As a teenager I used to come out here and hang over the railings, usually when dad was having a smoke, just to be near him because these journeys were always liberally punctuated with little trips to be somewhere other than with us, and I'd gaze down at the filthy water and be revolted, yet find it impossible to look away. Usually someone would stagger out of the door from the bar and vomit, either making it to the railing and casting their half-digested lunch into the waves, or just liberally sprinkling it about the deck, and either way it was nowhere near as horrifying as the water below. The English Channel is a necessary evil, something which must be tolerated in order to leave one land mass and reposition yourself on another land mass. Anyone who chooses to spend any more time than strictly necessary on these waters must be dangerously unhinged. The front of the boat is a far more pleasant and hopeful place to stand, particularly so as the chalky hulk of France starts to get closer and closer until you can start to make out individual houses and cars and people and the welcoming minutiae of everyday life, endless people who don't give a shit about you and the ferry you're on, just getting on with their lives. It's a view filled with hope.

But we always stood at the back, because there was less wind and it was easier to smoke. And so I stand at the back now, yearning for the hope but unable to claw my way towards it.

The French motorways are far, far better than I remember them being when I was a kid. I haven't been this way for, ooh, twenty years? More? And they always seemed to be a mess of confusing signs and rutted surfaces, not that I was paying much attention, it used to be a fourteen-hour drive down to Sauveterre-de-Rouergue so the best thing to do was pop my headphones on and try to sleep the whole way, but the road surface today is glassy smooth and all the signs look shiny and new. I remember mum saying years ago that they'd opened up a bunch of new motorways and it wasn't necessary to go the winding route through all the hills any more, and it was more like ten hours these days, which is quite a time saving but still sounds like a lot. It's 2 o'clock now, which means it's actually 3 o'clock French time, and can I push on through till after midnight? I can give it a go, I guess. I'd had a flick through the car's manual as we were waiting to disembark and I think I've sort of figured out the satnav. It reckons Sauveterre is about eight hours away, which sounds remarkably good, and hasn't the world moved on since the 1990s? But no, hang on… shit, I've put the wrong Sauveterre in. Delete, delete, delete. Good thing I checked, or I'd be halfway to Montpellier by now. Right, OK, nine hours and fifty-three minutes. That sounds bang on.

Christ though, motorways are boring, aren't they? Miles and miles and miles of endless dreary tarmac, white lines flashing by in a relentless stream like a super-slo-mo version of that bit in *Spaceballs* when they go to ludicrous speed, ankle set at just the right angle to keep the car at exactly 110km/h (which the speedo helpfully tells me is about 70mph), because the signs say both 110 and 130 and I've never understood why that is and now there's no-one to ask, I mean I could ask mum but she won't answer, and my ankle aches and I bet this car has cruise-control but fuck knows how you're supposed to make it work, and my back aches and my arse is numb and my nose is still throbbing and this is horrible. But things were markedly more horrible a few hours ago, and my god I can't believe the state of Jed's Crocodile Dundee boots, and I could be lying dead in the park with the remnants of my bacon sandwich being pecked off my corpse by inquisitive pigeons, and really this situation isn't so bad. The only thing the world's asking of me right now is to sit still and keep this vast machine between the white lines, and things could certainly be a lot more unpleasant. It's fine.
This journey really didn't seem so arduous when I was a kid, although that may well have been down to the fact that I was unconscious for most of it. My principal concern back then was running out of AA batteries for my Walkman, and there was that one time that it chewed up the tape I'd recorded for the trip that had *Dookie* on one side and *Smash* on the other and I had to come to terms with the fact that I'd be spending the holiday without my two new favourite albums, but aside from that it was largely stress-free, and really not too boring. Being the grown-up in the front puts rather a different spin on things. You can't just have a kip while you're in charge of two tonnes of speeding metal, it isn't the done thing. I'd like to though, I'd really like to, I can feel my body caving in, woozily, sinking into the darkening abyss of tiredness, suddenly jerking awake and realising the speedo needle has dropped to 40mph and I'm straddling two lanes,

perking up momentarily, desperately seeking a focal point that offers a little more hope than the endlessly shifting horizon. The white lines though, they're hypnotic. There's no way I can make it all the way there in one hit, I can feel my eyelids starting to sag. What time is it? 10pm. Can't be far off, surely, although I don't have any idea which of the numbers on the screen is my estimated time of arrival, and Christ I'm tired, and I'll just pull into this aire and have a doze. Just a quick one. Park between the truckers, they'll all be having a doze too. No problem with that. I'll stick the seat-warmer on. Probably won't need it on mum's side.

Chapter Eleven

The responsibility of holding the keys is awesome. Trust. So much trust in me, so it seems at least, earned over six solid years of service. I first started here as a broom-boy, or that appears to be the memory I have, it's a little hazy, sweeping the floor of the diner as well as acting as occasional security when the clientele got rowdy. But this isn't that kind of place, not really, the customers are generally pretty cool, the regulars in particular, and when they started calling me by name I knew I was in the club.

"I wanna talk to you," Sal had said, a couple of weeks back, over the feverish hubbub about the Orioles clinching the World Series, something I was pretty gassed about because I'd slung a few bucks on them, and Sal hardly ever wants to talk to anyone about anything so I knew it was either going to be something real bad or real good. And I knew there was no way he could've known about me and the guys from the kitchen selling cigarettes out the back door, because we made sure the truck only came on Thursdays, as Sal never works Thursdays, that's when he has his AA meeting, and our customers knew when the truck was coming and they always turned up right on time.

He'd clapped me on the back like my father never did, and handed me the keys to the diner. "You're opening up tomorrow," he said. "You've earned it, kid."

And I've been opening up every day since. Sixteen days of feeling like I own the damn place. Sure, there's a rota so me and all the other guys can take it in turns to open up, but those assholes don't want to be up that early in the morning. So the privilege is mine, all mine, to arrive at 5:30am, swing open the huge glass doors for the first of many times each day, the little bell going fuckin' ting-a-ling, flip up the light switches, turn on the grills, start setting out the ingredients in the kitchen, and for that precious half-hour before I turn the sign from *'Gee, we're closed'* to *'Sure, we're open'*, I can pretend that the whole place is mine. That I'm somebody, that I've made it.

If I can get all the setting up done in good time, I can make myself a filter coffee and sit on the customer side of the counter, and just enjoy a cup of joe like a regular joe for a minute, looking up at the tiles on the ceiling above the counter, the peach squares intersected by the white and blue and peach diamonds, and tracing patterns in the spilled coffee drops on the fresh new Formica counter-top. Sal likes to renew the surfaces on a regular basis, he reckons that clean furnishings imply clean food and that's what keeps people coming back. He has the red vinyl on the seats in the cubicles retrimmed every eighteen months too. He says steam-cleaning it doesn't go deep enough. His obsession with getting clean creeps into every corner of his life.

The bell over the door ding-a-lings about twenty seconds after I've flipped to *'Sure, we're open'*, and of course it's Marie, she's in first thing, regular as clockwork, short-stack of johnnycakes and a fresh OJ on the way to her shift at the market. And Bill, he's never far behind, making eyes at Marie along the counter as he ploughs his way through a double-serving of bacon and eggs. Always orders the toast, never eats it. And while he's chowing down on those eggs I know it's time to slap a couple of patties on the grill, the hot fat dancing around them, as more often than not we'll be seeing Jules before long, and he's a guy who doesn't fuck about when it comes to breakfast.

This is it. This is what I always wanted. My own little slice of the apple-pie dream.

We get our share of bikers in here, like every roadside diner always will, but when a shiny new Harley rumbles into the parking lot it's still an event, and everyone turns to the vista of floor-to-ceiling windows to see who's coming in, the kids standing on tippy-toes and separating the blinds with their little fingers. And this one? I don't know much about this kind of thing, but this one looks to be something special. "Say, that's the new Electra Glide," beams Richie, who felt the ground shaking and popped his head around the kitchen door for a look-see. "That a good one?"

"Boy howdy. Chromed to all get-out and packin' that Panhead."

"Ain't a Panhead, kid," says a new guy at the counter, we haven't been acquainted yet, he just came in for coffee. "That there's the Shovelhead motor."

They both nod in mutual appreciation that this must be a good thing, and by this time the rider's made it across the parking lot, between the slumbering lorry drivers and that weird European sedan that showed up from somewhere overnight, removing his helmet as he approaches the door, and goddamn it but it ain't a he, it's a she, and she shakes her hair out as she strolls between the red benches and sits herself up at the counter, bold as brass.

"Ma'am."

"Howdy, son. Y'all got good coffee here?"

"Best damn coffee in the State."

"That a fact?"

"Er… nope. But it's the best damn coffee in the room."

"That'll work, son, that'll work just fine."

There's a knack, I've found, to preparing the eggs just the way Bill likes 'em. Not that he'd care either way, I kinda get the feeling that he'd eat them even if he'd seen me drop them on the floor, but there's a lot of value to be placed in taking pride in your work. And it helps me continue the early morning feeling just a little longer, taking a bit of time over the details, doing things the way I would if I owned the place. Hell, maybe if I treat everybody nice then Sal will write me into the scene one day, let me take over when it comes time for him to hang up his bootlace tie. Maybe I just like to take my mind off of life. Anyway, what I do is crack three eggs into a bowl, and dash in just a tiny bit of sesame oil. Just a splash, nothing to overwhelm the flavour, just something to give it a bit of edge. A good hard whisking to make sure there's no chance of getting lumps, but not too much so that it starts to turn into a fuckin' meringue. Sprinkle in a little dill and some cracked black pepper, give it another stir for luck, then toss the lot into a sizzling hot pan with just a little olive oil. Now, we don't use olive oil as a rule, the place'd go under in days, but for my eggs, Bill's eggs, the cheap sunflower shit just won't do. You gotta keep it moving in the pan, round and round and up and down, but don't brown it, don't overcook it, just let it crumble into cartoon birdfeed and slap it on the plate. Tear up some basil leaves and sprinkle them on top, and Bill's a happy man.

"Yo, where's the bacon?"

Shit. See, I never said I was a cordon bleu chef.

The Harley chick's been coming in pretty regularly over the last couple of weeks, near enough every day, and she has a knack of arriving just when I have a little time to spare. So we get to talking, about how come she's got such a meaty bike, how come a lady of her, you know, background, is out and about on a Harley at all, and how she's had to deal with that stupid fuckin' question every day since the thirties.

"Name's Bessie," she'd said on that first day, after draining her second cup of coffee, her white jodhpurs and baby blue boots matching the tiling under the counter almost as precisely as they matched the Electra Glide outside. "They called me the Motorcycle Queen of Miami. Taught myself to ride an Indian back when I was knee-high to who-knows-what, and rode that beautiful machine all over the South."

A couple of days ago we'd been talking about childhood and fairgrounds, and today she's brought a photograph to show me. It's her, sepia-tinted and without quite so many years on her, standing beside a big sign that says 'Wall of Death'.

"Y'all used to watch the stunt riders?"

"Honey, I *was* a stunt rider. How d'you think a young black woman of no certain means makes a buck in the South? Man, most folks wouldn't even let me sleep inside. But I had a bike, and if you've got a bike then you can make a buck. Folks'll pay you to do anything if there's a chance you might die while they watch – spinnin' around in that wall of death, riding along the carnival parade standing on the handlebars, hanging off the back of the saddle…"

"Ha, you should go out there and give us a show, Bessie! All these fellas in here would throw a few dollars into the hat for that shit."

Nods of agreement ripple along the counter.

"These days? No, that kinda business is long behind me. Besides kid, I don't come in here to pay my bills, I'm doin' just fine thank you."

"I bet Bill would just love to race you. His daddy bought him a Topper, that'll max out at 45mph if he lays off the eggs."

"Hey, shut the fuck up," Bill laughs.

"You know I did used to race," says Bessie. "Back on the dirt tracks, that was another way to make a little scratch. Course, you needed a proxy to collect the winnings, there's no way they'd pay out if they saw me take my helmet off and found a damn woman, a damn *black* woman inside it."

"Damn fuckin' straight," says a new guy sitting at the corner of the counter. "Creature like you ain't got no place there. Fuckin' disgrace." I didn't like the look of him when he stumbled in, and I'm really not liking the look of him now. Arrogant motherfucker.

Bessie turns back to her coffee, eyes downcast with the weight of ages. I grab the pot and give her a top-up, and Bill eyeballs the stranger warily as he chews on his eggs.

"Shouldn't even be in here now, specially not sitting at the counter with the white folks like you're fuckin' special," the guy goes on, and for a moment looks as if he might spit on the floor before thinking better of it.

"Hey, easy buddy, there's no call for that here."

"No fuckin' *call* for it? These animals, they think they can do whatever the fuck they want? Hell, no! Bitch, my daddy used to keep one of your kind for suckin' dick and sweepin' the damn porch."

"Hey! You want me to throw your ass outta here? I won't be having that kinda talk in here, this is your last warning."

"Fuck you man, you think I'm the one with the problem? Fuckin' minstrel show over here, we used to chase the likes of that shit right outta the county! Cops over the line would round 'em up for DWB, the ol' Drivin' While Black, makes me fuckin' *sick* seein' her sat here like it's all dandy and roses. This the sort of behaviour you allow in your place? Should be ashamed of yourself son, fuckin' ashamed."

"That's it," I say banging the counter lid open and grabbing him by the arm, "Bill, gimme a hand getting this jerkoff outta here." The smell of cordite is a sensory overload, almost as much as the physical sensation of a hot bullet penetrating soft and yielding flesh, and I can't believe I hadn't spotted the matching gang jackets until now. The stranger's buddy, sitting over in the corner, sports a perfect John Wayne stance as he levels the pistol precisely at where Bill's head had been until a moment before. It's amazing how quickly everyone dives to the floor, a diner full of people suddenly seemingly empty, and the only faces I see are the stranger's, and his buddy's, and Bessie staring straight ahead, and my own reflection in the stainless steel cooler at the end of the counter. The stranger pulls out a piece of his own and casually, coolly, resting his elbows on the Formica, aims the muzzle squarely at Bessie's temple. And man, she doesn't even react, she just keep staring straight ahead like someone who's seen this shit time and time again.

"Alrighty then," says the other, "since we've got ourselves a little situation here we might as well make something of it. You, peckerwood, hand me a trash bag."

I do, unable to think of an alternative.

"OK, then. Ladies and gentlemen, this appears to have turned into a robbery," he leers. "I'm going to come around with this trash bag, and you're all going to drop your wallets and purses into it. Watches too. Anyone gives me any shit, you're giving me your wedding rings. Anyone gives me any *real* shit, and you can just take a look at this dead piece of shit on the floor over here."

He turns to gesture his gun at Bill, but Bill's gone.

"What the…?"

And the stranger's face colourfully erupts, the force of the bullet entering the back of his head causing the pulpy mush of his brain to fan out of his face like a blossoming lily, and as he slumps over the counter into a soup of his own gore Bill's standing right behind him, an ear hanging off but still looking statuesque as he pivots to aim at the guy holding the sack, snuffing him out instantly with impeccable precision.

"Y'all should know better than to fuck with a farm boy at breakfast time," he says, and for a moment I can't help wondering whether he's said that line quite a lot of times before in imaginary scenarios in his mind.

The customers are fleeing, running like hell, and Richie's calling the police from the payphone on the far wall, and there's bits of brain all over my shiny counter, but it isn't my fucking counter is it, it never will be, this is exactly the kind of thing that happens if you let yourself believe that everything's alright, and Bessie's left a five on the counter and there's a rooster-tail of dust behind the Harley as she rumbles off into the desert. I wonder how much of her life she's spent running.

Chapter Twelve

There's a horrible shock when you do that waking-with-a-start thing, sitting bolt upright and breathing in sharply, as you've been breathing shallowly and gently all night and then suddenly you've forced your lungs to work much harder without notice. They don't like it. Mine don't, anyway. Seems unfair, I haven't smoked in years. Aren't those little alveoli supposed to regenerate?

Shit, it has been all night too. What time did I get here, ten o'clock? And now it's eight in the morning and I genuinely don't think I've ever needed a piss this much in my entire life. The truckers are gone and I'm alone in the lorry park, a suspiciously steamed-up saloon, the dawn sun glinting off the dew on the bonnet like a thousand tiny nuggets of amber. I allow myself a moment's satisfied pause to consider that, of all the places in the world, Jed's unlikely to be looking for me here. But there's no time to ponder this as I really am going to wee all over the car if I don't act with a certain degree of haste, so I try to open the door but it won't open and there's no obvious reason why and why the fuck has it locked itself and do I need to press a button or something, Christ, but on the second pull all the doors click and I tumble out onto the tarmac with, it has to be said, rather less finesse than I'd ideally like. Every muscle, every joint is seized in place – but hey, at least I didn't have to shell out for a hotel room – as I stagger across the improbably vast parking area toward the toilet block, delighted to find that it contains a real actual lavatory rather than the hellish ceramic squattie that would always be waiting to disappoint you when we used to make this journey back in the nineties, and I unleash what feels like my entire body weight in fluid, and bloody hell it's all over my shoes. Bollocks. But no, it's fine, I mean I can rinse them in the sink and dry them under the hand dryer and it's OK, really, in the grand scheme of things having widdled on your trainers isn't life-changingly awful.

There's piss all over the floor out there too of course, not my piss, just general French piss, so the act of removing my shoes to rinse them has the air of an *Inbetweeners* caravan park mishap about it, so instead I opt to go outside and just shuffle my feet through the long grass because that's probably fine and sod it, there's no-one around anyway so what does it matter?

And then *fuck*, there he is, there's Jed, *what the fuck*, he's coming out of the petrol station, cracking open an energy drink and heading towards a... wait, no, what would Jed be doing in France driving an old van? And no, it definitely isn't him, he's too short and his nose is the wrong shape and the hair's far too long, and what am I doing to myself, but fuck this, I have to get out of here, and I realise I'm running, sprinting for all I'm worth, out-of-shape legs like ocean liner pistons, and I yank open the BMW's door, which is heavy, why does it need to be so heavy, I bet it's full of motors, and I press the stupid fucking variety of buttons required to get the stupid fucking thing working and floor the throttle and just power across the grass toward the slip road because Christ I have to get away, this is too intense, too weird, and it can't have been him, there's no way it was him, but I have to go, I have to be gone, and 155mph seems to be all this car can do and I don't know if that's good or bad for a modern car but it doesn't feel fast enough and please, please, just pull that horizon toward me.

French villages and rural towns have a sleepiness which I don't think will ever change. You can add as many satellite dishes and solar panels and new cars and modern shop signs as you like into the picture, and it'll still always be 1949, the poor but wholly content locals going about their daily business, taking produce to market, stopping off for a pastis, fulfilling any number of other Gallic clichés concerning boules and baguettes and wildly flailing cages of chickens, seemingly unaware that the place they inhabit is an idyllic picture postcard for any passing Brit. It's just their home. That's what houses look like. There's no sense that any of their surroundings are remarkable. It's one of my favourite things about rural France, there's a gorgeous lack of self-awareness.

It's amazing how quickly the geography comes flooding back. I haven't been here since the Britpop wars, and yet everything's immediately familiar. Time creaks along here. These streets, man, I remember running through these streets with the French kids, taunting the ducks in the long pond, bunnyhopping our BMXs through the bastide arches around the square, Madame Dupont chasing us away from the café with her broom as we knocked over her chairs with our bikes, selfish as kids are. It feels very weird to be *driving* into the town. That's what grown-ups do. That's what dad always did, ratty as hell by this point after the endless slog through the hills, me and mum elated to have finally reached the end point of the epic journey. I glance across at her and smile. "Here we are, ma. Home."

I don't think I've ever consciously called it that before. It wasn't technically home of course, just holiday-home, but this was the happy place, the place without the shouting or the moods, the place with less stress, where we could just get on and not think about life. The place of pastis and barbecues, card games and static-crackling *Monty Python* videos. Silliness and safety and simple living.

I head under the arch and up the Rue Saint Christophe, not because it's the quickest route but because I suddenly want to see the square with every fibre of my being, and as I turn right past the arches it's every bit as wonderful as I remember, and I immediately regret heading down the side road past the church because this car is huge and this town wasn't really built for 21st-century transport, and I s-q-u-e-e-z-e between the scarred rocks as the lady from the wine store scowls at my obvious ignorance, and I really can't say I blame her. I'll come back and investigate the town later, this is layering a sheen of stress over my idyllic memories and nobody needs that, it's fine, I'll come back later, I just need to direct this barge out of town and up Les Safranières, out into the woods.

And there it is. The house. Home. Not overgrown as I was expecting; in fact, not too dissimilar to how I remember it from when I last saw it. It feels like the nineties, it's like I've just driven into my memories. How can that be?

The front of the house appears well groomed, which is a strange way to consider a house, but the creepers and passion flowers used to totally envelope the stairs up to the front door, we'd always have to machete our way in when we arrived after a long absence, it was one of the horrifying inevitabilities of the long journey down. After all that time in the car you'd be bursting for a wee, and yet you couldn't just run in and use the loo because you'd first have to go down into the cellar and get the machetes, and isn't it weird that in the French countryside it's not unusual to own things like machetes and shotguns, in suburban Britain such things would get you banged up, and we'd have to hack down all the foliage up the steps in order to even reach the front door. And yet today it all looks neatly manicured, and impressively tidy, tidier than it ever did when I used to come here although that was a lifetime ago, and that just doesn't make any sense at all.

Thankfully the hiding place for the spare key is still as it always was, inside the false fire extinguisher in the cellar, as I hadn't had time to hunt down mum's keys before leaving the house. And as I turn the key in the Yale lock and ease the heavy oak door open I'm intrigued to find… a light on. And music playing on the stereo, *'Ooh, your life, ooh, it may be a dream, hey hey, baby it's OK, just let it all go and float away'*, and through the back door's strangely clean window pane I can see a woman mowing the lawn. I have no idea who she is. This is all extremely unsettling. Yep, the fridge has milk and cheese in it too, and the logpile by the fireplace is topped up. It's starting to feel like there's every chance I'm still asleep in the aire and this is all just a despair-inducing fantasy, and yet as the woman comes up the stairs to the back door she throws reality into sharp focus by breaking into a half-run when she sees me, beaming a magnificent smile, and it becomes apparent that it's Madame Aznavour from the house by the church, she's got a few years on her but those dimples haven't faded, and she tumbles into the house with an effusive "Ah, jeunehomme, depuis combien de temps je t'ai vu?" and she's grabbing my shoulders and how many kisses do they do again, two, three, four, but it's OK, she's taking the lead, *kiss*, *kiss*, *kiss*, and Christ I've forgotten all my French. She's gabbling at me like a lunatic and how long is it since I actually spoke French to anyone, and a lot of it's sinking in but it's taking me longer than I'd like to process it all, so by the time I've managed to formulate a response she's moved onto another topic, and fucking hell slow down woman, this is bewildering. I was expecting an empty house. I think. I don't know what I was expecting. But she's grabbed her bag and proffered an "À toute à l'heure!" and scampered off down the front steps and I don't think I managed to even get a word in. Bloody hell.

The wine cellar is still impressively well stocked, and it feels deliciously naughty to be able to go down there and simply pluck out a bottle for myself at will, ignoring the rotation of vintages and scribbled chart of drink-by dates and simply easing out a 1994 Cuvée Prestige because I remember that being a good one, all oaky and rich and warm. Settling into the weathered armchair on the terrace, swirling the Syrah-rich Gaillac around a glass to observe its legs, I try to piece together what it was Madame Aznavour had been saying. It seemed as if she was expecting mum to come back at some point, and she'd been keeping the house nice for her, and something about expecting her at this time of year and being surprised not to see her last year, and some information about a new grandson or something that I couldn't really figure out. All of which seems very odd, as surely mum, like me, hasn't been back here for decades? It was dad's place really, when he left us we stopped coming here, and anyway mum has her annual summer trip with her friend Jude, she goes to stay with her for a couple of months and...

And I'm a fucking idiot. She's been coming here all along, hasn't she? Coming here to the site of the only truly happy memories I have. Without me. Why wouldn't she tell me this?

<hr />

Existence – it's a multifaceted thing, is it not? Consider, on the one hand, just how lucky you are to exist. That's what we're always told. Endlessly. We're so damn lucky to be here. Life, it supposedly goes without saying, is something to be cherished; when you think about your existence in mathematical terms, the likelihood of you being here at all is phenomenally small. Your parents were feeling amorous on that particular night nine months prior to your birth, and of all those sticky little swimmers, you were the one that got through and made it to the egg. And as if those numbers weren't mind-boggling enough, their parents did the same, and their parents, and their parents... when you follow the thread all the way back through the timeline of humanity – or, if you wish to stretch it yet further, through the evolution of all multi-cellular life forms, or even right back to the Big Bang – the chances of there being one of you, right here, right now, are really very small indeed. Well done. You made it. So, what did you – a general 'you' – traditionally do to celebrate this tremendous good fortune? Sit there on the sofa in your pants, eating a massive bag of Doritos and watching an episode of *The Big Bang Theory* that you've seen three times before? C'mon, that's not what your grandfather shot a Nazi in the face for is it, that's not why that diplodocus sneezed, that's not why that single-celled protozoa started thinking about morphing with others to form clusters. Get out there and look at the world, that's what we're told, it's huge, and every part of it is the product of just as many mind-boggling coincidences as you are. Your legacy will resonate through the ages. You only get to do this once. Think about the entire lifespan of planet Earth, compared to your own really quite short life. You will never, ever get to do this again. Make the most of it! Have fun! Look at stuff! Achieve things that your great-grandchildren will be proud to tell their friends about!

Fuck that. Fuck the positivity. Life doesn't especially want us here. Yes, it is staggeringly impressive in statistical terms that you – specifically, *you* – came to exist. But don't be too impressed with yourself, it's not like you're the only human who managed it. You are not unique, you're just one of many. There are several billion other people who got there too, most of whom couldn't give a shit about your enthusiasm over the probability of it all. You are a meaningless speck in space-time. The human race will eventually die out, that's a certainty, and the planet will boil away into oblivion. Take a step back and look at the Earth from space, slowly rotating regardless of your actions, the universe just getting on with things - you play *no* part in this, you're a grain of sand in an infinite hourglass. Humanity as a species is a disease upon a rock that would be in much better shape without us. When you think about the age of the universe, years become largely irrelevant; what's a million years in relation to the solar system? Chicken feed. But a million years to the human race? Where will we be in a million years' time? Nowhere, that's where. Extinct. Cosmically speaking, we'll be of very little consequence – as important as the ice they found on Mars, or the glimmering tail of a comet; little more than an oh-that's-interesting diversion. Nothing you do today means a single damn thing. So what if you forgot to eat breakfast or record *EastEnders*, or your roof's leaking, or you've got a headache, or your dad left you and someone tried to kill you on a bridge and your car got stolen and a psychotic ex-colleague wants to stab you up? Nobody cares, the universe doesn't give a shit. In the grand scheme of humanity, none of this has any value. I suppose the best thing you can do is just try not to be too much of a dick. But when the only person in the world you thought you could trust has been habitually lying to you? Fuck it. Just fuck it all. None of this, nothing matters.

It's surprisingly easy to slip into a new routine, and I have to say I feel supremely relaxed. After the first couple of days disappeared in wine I managed to make the walk into Sauveterre to stock up on supplies, the dialect has always been slightly Spanish-sounding here, their 'pain' is pronounced 'peng', and on returning to the house it occurred to me to check out the state of the pool. Yes, Madame Aznavour has been keeping the filter running and the chemicals in check, so this has pretty much become my life now. Get up, stick a croissant under the grill, put a pot of coffee on, perhaps curl up in a ball and shudder away the terror that Jed might be somewhere out there because he definitely isn't, I mean surely, dust myself down and enjoy my light breakfast, then while away the day swimming, sipping *vin rouge*, snacking on cheese, and being the man of the house. The evenings are the best bit. I can live out those joyful memories from my early teens, except with the roles shifted so that I'm the one in charge, I'm making the decisions. I can fire up the raclette, sizzle some sliced-up saucisson and ooze a bit of melty cheese into a crispy baked potato, and I can do that every night because who's going to tell me it's not a good idea? I can give myself a tour of the wines, drinking chronologically or by cépage or simply choosing at random, and snuggle up in the big armchair, the one that was always his armchair, and have the best view of the TV, and drunkenly laugh myself stupid at old *Red Dwarf* videos, because the world may have moved on since the 1990s but I certainly didn't bloody ask it to. Tonight I'm working through Series VI and a rather splendid Passion Doux, which I know is a pudding wine meant to be enjoyed chilled and in tiny quantities, but I'm the man of the house here and I'll glug it warm by the damn pint if I want to, and I'd forgotten how magnificently well scripted this show was. *"Sir, are you absolutely sure? It does mean changing the bulb…"*
A knock on the front door wrenches me from my reverie. I really don't want to talk to anyone. This little routine has become so

comfortable. I can honestly say I don't have a care in the world. Perhaps if I ignore it, they'll go away.

But there's the knock again, a little more insistent this time. I curse the nature of centuries-old oak doors for their lack of modern spyholes, that's the sort of innovation that just makes sense and rustic France would be a safer place with just a slightly keener awareness of domestic security, most of these people don't even lock their doors when they go to the shops, and who can it be at this time of night, it's gone ten o'clock, and as I swing the door open I'm some level beyond gobsmacked to find that it's him. How on earth did he find me here?

"It wasn't too much of a stretch to track you down," says Wilson, as he pours us both a generous pastis. "Your front door had been smashed in when I came to speak to you a week ago, and the house had been turned upside down, every room was a mess."

I nod dumbly.

"This doesn't come as a surprise to you? OK, well, we'd been looking into your family records to try to ascertain a little background anyway, you know, throughout the various unpleasantnesses we've collectively encountered recently, and there are numerous records of your mother coming here. Seems she makes an annual trip of it?"

"I suppose so."

"You didn't come with her? Seems odd, sir, if you don't mind me saying? Given how close you were, I mean."

"Yes. It does seem fucking odd, doesn't it?"

He holds my gaze for a beat longer than is comfortable. "Quite. So anyway, with your friend Jed back in custody I thought it prudent to seek you out. Your sudden departure was a little concerning. Looks like this hunch rather paid off."

I knock back the pastis in one and he refills it without prompt, just like the barman on the boat, and is that just what people do these days? If so, I like it. Say all you want about society and culture going down the drain, it's behavioural developments like this that keep us all civilised.

"You've rearrested him?"

"Well, yes and no. Sort of separately arrested him, if you like. He's nothing to do with the terror attack, I think we all know that…"

Christ, stop looking at me like that.

"…but we arrested him for a separate offence."

"What did he do?"

"He pulled a knife on a taxi driver. A very big one."

"Oh. What was very big, the knife or the taxi driver?"

Wilson takes a hearty pull of his saccharine aniseed. "The knife," he deadpans.

I swirl the remnants of my ice cube around in the half-millimetre of pastis that remains in the bottom of the glass, momentarily losing myself in the beauty of its diminishing mass, gently eroding into the liquid until there's nothing left of it at all. It's such a clear memory that's so closely associated with this house, you don't realise as a kid quite how much time you spend focusing on ice cubes in glasses, and for a second, just a second, I want to throw myself onto the lawn and weep at the loss of those glorious, endlessly happy days. Everything was so simple. Before dad walked out on us and ripped all these memories to shreds.

I know exactly how big that knife is, thank you.

"It's quite late, officer. Do you have somewhere to stay?"

"Brian, please. No, I don't, but I think I saw a hotel in the square on my way in?"

"The Hotel de Ville?"

"That's the one."

"Ah, not a hotel. It means 'town hall'."

"Oh. I probably shouldn't try to sleep there, then."

"There's plenty of bedrooms here, officer, you're welcome to stay. The one at the end there has an en suite. And the water pressure's really good, you get a great shower here. And I've bought supplies, there's a smashing butcher in the town, and a brilliant greengrocer who grows most of his own produce, and the bakery is incredible, it really is, you'll love the *pain rustique*, I'll slice some up for us in the morning, and the melons from the market are just perfect, and…"

"OK, OK, take it easy. Let's have another drink. And yes, thank you, it would be very convenient to stay."

I don't know at which point I'd managed to slip back into the desperate-to-please-teenager role, he's only been here about twenty minutes, but I'm pretty sure I'm OK with it. There's something reassuring about Wilson's commanding stance and the unwavering focus of his gaze, he just… fits in here. With mum here too it's almost a complete picture.

Shit. Mum's on the mantlepiece. Has he noticed? That might look weird, bringing her with me. I'll sneak her out when he goes to the loo or something.

I stand and reach across the table for the pastis bottle, suddenly aware that my legs aren't as solid as they had been earlier, it's the curse of drinking a lot while sitting down, it's only when you stand up that your equilibrium goes to cock, and by that point there's no turning back. The wonky oak floorboards have risen and fallen and settled over the centuries, and as I sit back down one of the chair legs slips down a gap between two boards and catapults me to the floor where, in my subconscious keenness to save the bottle I'm still holding, I don't put my arms out to break my fall and thus take a faceful of oak that's hardened like iron, and my nose which has been healing nicely bursts chaotically all over the astounded Wilson's shoes. I grab hold of the table to try and raise myself up and, ha, save face, but the tablecloth decides to piss all over this bright idea and extravagantly showers me with glasses and water from the jug and peanuts from the little dish that I made in Year Nine ceramics and I was always very proud that they actually found a use for, and *fuck it all* I'm not having this, so I let go of the bottle and push myself to my feet, immediately slipping over in the spilled water and landing arse-first in the graceless little puddle of my nose-blood.

Jesus, and why's he laughing, the bastard?

"I'm sorry, but you really should see yourself," he chuckles, with a tone that immediately makes me forgive him, and just for a split-second I hope he stays forever. "I think you'd better get yourself to bed, hadn't you?"

A rhetorical question, of course, and as I slink away he heads off in the opposing direction to the end bedroom, and through the thick but ill-sealed and draughty door I can hear him abluting in the en suite. I mean, I'm sure all of that was fine, it's not embarrassing because there was clearly a funny side, he was laughing *with* me wasn't he, and my nose was already injured beforehand so I don't need to worry too much about that. I tiptoe out, very wobbly, which is OK, it's a wobbly floor so that's probably actually stabilising me a bit, and grab the urn off the mantle, sneaking mum into my room and installing her on the dresser instead. Smart, I think.

He looks so different to how he did on the bridge, crisp in his pressed uniform, slightly harassed by the necessary urgency of terror.

This bed has always been comfortable, I wonder if it's had a lot of use over the last couple of decades, because it feels just like it used to do, and the light fitting in the ceiling is like a wormhole in space as it transports me back to the time when I was fifteen and got alcohol poisoning from a family wedding where everyone took turns to break me in with pint after pint after pint, and I ended up lying here and staring at that light fitting for what felt like days. Probably was days, I have no idea. Five silver globes, each with a protruding light bulb, with one globe having a slightly matt finish in contrast to the other chromed ones, and I wondered whether it was a deliberate design idea, but why would you do that, or a bored factory worker being mischievous with the sandpaper, or maybe just the fact that it was cheap. Inconsequential musings, stretched out over (possibly) several immobile teenage days. I know that light fitting better than I know most people. Seeing it again erases all of the time between now and then. A constant. A reassuring constant.

Yes, he did look different on the bridge. And I realise that I haven't run through the events on the bridge in my mind since; it's usually my way to obsess, to pick over detail, to run through events over and over to give myself a clear impression of what other people saw of me, how I might have been judged, how they might be seeing me the next time we meet, but I suppose the events of that day were so patently not about me specifically that it felt fraudulent to dwell.

So what did happen? I was walking across the bridge, I remember that very clearly, the muddle of wine and pastis can't do anything to blur the edges of that memory. I suspect that will never diminish, it's hewn in the granite of my mind. The stark angularity of the concrete architecture, the hum of the pleasure boat passing below, the excited yelps of the teenagers down at the end of the bridge practising their parkour over the steps down to the South Bank, the summery crispness in the air, the colossal relief of another day ticked off the list and the magnificent feeling of heading away from work rather than towards it.

The grinding of metal on metal. The squeal and acrid stench of tortured rubber. The shower of sparks, almost cartoonish, like something improbable from a movie. The tiny cubes of smashed safety glass tinkling over the chunky bolts of that oh-so-sturdy barrier. The reassuringly knobbly feel of my knees pushing into my chest as I made myself as small as I could physically be. That smell of cordite, so weirdly familiar in spite of a total lack of precedent or context. The shriek of bullets ripping the air; the shriek of humans transmogrifying into macabre puppets of meat, their souls ushered away by vicious malice. A blinding red flash through my closed eyelids bringing a sudden feeling of calmness, finality, serenity. The glint of sky as I open my eyes, as if being reborn, the familiarity of the ozone rendered momentarily slapstick by the sight of a body arcing across it. It's so crisp, so clear. I feel as if I'm still there, like I never left. As if that day, the day I've subconsciously refused to picture since, has drawn me back into its irresistible state of limbo.

Chapter Thirteen

"It's a shot tower," says the newspaper seller, in a tone which suggests I'm the stupidest person he's met that day, which is of course entirely possible. The vista here seems strangely alien to what I'm expecting, which isn't really helping with my own perspective on what sort of grasp I have on the world today; the most immediately noticeable thing is the lack of scaffolding around Big Ben, although why would I think there should be scaffolding there, had they been cleaning the clock faces recently or something? I really should pay more attention. And then there's the glaring hole in the landscape across from the Elizabeth Tower, on the south side of the river, where there should be something tall and yet there demonstrably isn't, and I can't quite put my finger on what that is. And as I lean my elbows on the railings of the bridge, which feels much narrower than my mind tells me it should be and far less busy, and entirely the wrong shape come to think of it, I can't help but notice that there's markedly less concrete about the place than my memory is crying out for. And yet… no, it's always looked this way, hasn't it? Of course it has, how could it be any other way? And the bridge can't seem odd, as this has always been the bridge. That's just an immutable constant. This is the kind of nonsense a keen cup of tea should shake clear, I'm sure. For all the years I've been commuting to Waterloo and dodging in amongst the barrows and horses on the way to Covent Garden, this is the scenescape that's always greeted me, there's no question of that and I really can't explain this unwelcome sense of unease; edifices caked in Victorian blackness, a sweeping promenade of baked-in soot, and it occurs to me that I have no idea what the tower at the south end of the bridge is for. So I'd asked the newspaper seller. He seemed like the sort of switched-on character who'd be clued-up on such matters.

"I see. And what exactly is a shot tower?"

"Buy a newspaper and I'll tell you."

Fire wrecks Crystal Palace: Duke of Kent wears a fireman's helmet. It's an intriguing headline, certainly. How can you set fire to glass? It sounds very unlikely. That's got to be worth a penny of anyone's money.

"Cheers, guv'nor."

"So?"

"So what?"

"So what's a shot tower?"

"It's a tower where they make shots."

Shrug.

"You know, shots for shotguns."

"Ah, I see." He's keen to push off, I can tell by the way he's already done so, but that's fair enough, I can see how time is money in that profession.

The Ferris wheel, that's what's missing! But when has there been a Ferris wheel on the banks of the Thames, what am I thinking of? Must have been a fair or something, it's hazy. The edges of everything are a bit hazy, and I'm not sure I'm entirely happy about it. But it's probably fine really, I mean, isn't everything? There's a policeman directing traffic at the north end of the bridge, thick white cuffs covering his forearms, presumably with the aim of making him more visible to traffic, but actually giving him the impression of somebody who's bought a cheap and slightly unconvincing police uniform in a fancy dress shop, and his whirling arm movements are almost lost in a mass of canvas-sided vans, horse-drawn carriages of fruit and vegetables, and the ubiquitous Routemasters with their boasts of 'CHEAP MIDDAY FARES' and their chunkily-lettered adverts: *Guinness is good for you*; *Wrigley's – for vim and vigour*; *Haig Whisky – don't be vague, ask for Haig*. This is life-affirming stuff. I mean, it's probably a bit early for a Guinness, but if it's good for me…

I stop at Smith's Café on Covent Garden, instead opting for a nice cup of tea. Probably a more socially acceptable way to start the day. Besides, rubbing elbows with the other suits while honking of Guinness isn't the strongest look. I already have to fight through the ignominy of having left my hat on the tram, thus rendering myself quite possibly the only hatless man in London, and inevitably I've trodden in horse shit on the way here because there's always horse shit, that's just a facet of city living you cannot escape.

I like the anonymity of Smith's. It's such an uninspiring name for a café, and this lack of imagination is neatly mirrored in the menu, the décor, even the staff. There's a functionality to it all. You ask for a cup of tea, you get a cup of tea, no messing about. Bit of toast to go with it, but you'll have to wait for an egg, the man hasn't been yet. Can you not sit there sir, there's a leak. Lovely wholesomeness, it's like being casually ignored by your own family.

Waterloo Bridge's days are numbered, says page 4, and this triggers something in my brain that I can't quite place. A… an aching? I've felt this ache before, there's a finality to it, an unsettling glimpse into oblivion, but without any rational explanation of why.

I remember a theory from long ago about how one's life was connected by a long strand, one end attached to the place of your birth and the other to the site of your death; the strand could stretch and knot and tangle and twist, but as long as neither end point were detached, your life would always remain on a reasonably stable course. I feel as if someone is twanging my strand for sport.

'Sir Giles Gilbert Scott is the architect of the new Waterloo Bridge, due to be constructed on the site of the existing structure after its imminent demolition. Continuous beams will support a wide pair of spans on either side of the river, shaped to resemble arches in the classical style, all clad in Portland stone which will be cleansed by the rain; a shining light beacon among Waterloo's soot of industry.'

"How are we supposed to map this city if the council keep changing bits of it?" asks a voice beside me. A slightly wild-eyed woman is reading the newspaper over my shoulder, having inexplicably joined me at the table, but I suppose that's fine, it's a busy place. Well, it usually is, not so much this morning. But still.

"I'm sorry? Map the city?"

"Yes, you know draw maps. Note down where everything is."

"Of course. That's what you do, is it?"

"Why, I'm glad you asked." She flashes me a broad smile, two perfect rows of gleaming pearly-whites, and for a moment I lose myself in the clarity of her eyes. How quickly you can be distracted from this revolting city. Any flash of cleanliness immediately counterpoints the relentless grime and soot.

"Have you got time for a stroll?"

I glance at my pocket watch, and no, I don't have time to do any such thing, I'm close to running late as it is, but her magnificent forwardness is so beguiling that I can hardly refuse, can I?

"Absolutely, I'd be delighted, Miss…?"

"Pearsall. Call me Phyllis, please."

"Charmed. Shall we?"

But this last question is entirely redundant as she's already halfway to the door and I scamper after her, again briefly losing myself in the swirling grace of her perfume. It smells like violets.

Such a comforting aroma, I just want to be near it, enveloped in it. Ah, this life, it can be a dream.

"I want to tell you a story," she says, as she strides away from the cobbles of the Garden and downhill toward the Strand; I'm just about managing to keep up without panting like someone who's never before walked at pace.

"Oh, splendid. I like stories."

"Full disclosure first, however. I know who you are."

"I... I beg your pardon?"

"You work at WHSmith's headquarters, don't you? On Southampton Row? I've seen you going in there in the mornings. Are you important?"

"Well, I... that's not really for me to say."

"Do you make decisions?"

"Don't we all?"

She huffs a little, then collects herself, sitting on a bench outside the Savoy Theatre and motioning for me to sit beside her. "So then, my story," she says. "Three years ago, I found myself attending a party in Belgravia, and on the way there I became irretrievably lost."

I light a cigarette, proffering the silver case toward her. She takes one distractedly, producing a pocket lighter of her own as if from nowhere, and I'm impressed as much by the sleight of hand as the grace with which she carries it all off so seamlessly.

"The city was like a maze," she continues, exhaling delicately, her smoke somehow almost seeming to clean the sooty air around her for just a moment. The fusion of tobacco smoke and violets is certainly one that should be revisited, it's intoxicating.

"I determined there and then that the city needed to be mapped. And, furthermore, that I was the person to do it."

"But... surely the city has already been mapped? Quite a few times, in fact? Bartholomew's Reference Atlas, for example..."

"Not like this. This was to be utterly comprehensive, no alleyway or thoroughfare overlooked, no close or mews too big or too small, everything treated with equal importance and all fastidiously chronicled as much for the seasoned traveller as the first-time visitor."

"I see. That sounds like a fairly mammoth task."

"*Rem acu tetigisti*, my new friend, *rem acu tetigisti*. I walked, oh I walked and walked! A whole calendar year, eighteen-hour days, three thousand solid miles of walking, note-taking, getting everything perfectly noted and organised."

"But... why? I mean, you did this all by yourself? Surely it would have been quicker and easier to pay a few people to help you?"

"Pay them with what?"

"Ah."

"Sir, this was my mission, my vision. No obstacle could divert me from it. 23,000 streets, and I walked every single one."

"Is that... I mean, *really*? That's... I can't wrap my mind around the logistics of that. You were starting from the same point each day, or...?"

"My methods were my methods, sir, and after a full revolution of the sun and numerous pairs of boots, I had it completed, my cartographical *magnum opus*: the A-Z."

This final statement was somewhat muffled by a passing beer cart. "Sorry, the Hater's Head?"

"Ay-too-zed, sir, ay-too-zed."

"Because it covers all the streets from the first to the last, I see. Very clever."

I stub my cigarette out on the arm of the bench and pivot slightly to face her. "Listen, I need to be getting to the office, but perhaps we could finish your story over lunch?"

She looks as if I've just slapped her grandmother, but I'm again impressed by the remarkable swiftness with which she gathers herself together and rearranges her expression into one of pleasant blankness. "Of course. 12:30 at Smith's?"

"Wonderful. Thank you, Miss Pearsall, I shall see you then..."

...but she's already away, leaping onto the back of a Routemaster in the direction of Fleet Street, and I really should have clarified whether she meant we should meet at Smith's the café, or WHSmith's the office, where she thinks I work.

Where I *did* work. Until that little meeting happened. Before I was cast adrift into a futile commuting routine with no office hours to provide the filling in this pointless travelling sandwich.

The newspaper seller acts as if he's never seen me before, which is one of my favourite things about him. We go through this charade almost every morning, me offering a little chit-chat, him refusing to give up too much information until he's received his shiny penny and offloaded one of his papers, it's a merry little badinage we share and it's as if his memory wipes itself clean every time we part.

"Excuse me son, but have you ever heard of The London Eye?"

"What's that mister, some sort of fancy restaurant or something?"

"No, more of a landmark, I think. It… it rings a bell, but I can't fathom for why."

"Tell you what – buy a newspaper and I'll ask around for you."

"I have a newspaper," I say, needlessly waving the one he sold me just half an hour ago by way of unnecessary proof.

"Well then, I guess you're all set for having your curiosity satisfied right now, aint'cha?" he grins, and with that, as quickly as Miss Pearsall vaulting onto a bus, he's immediately gone and I'm alone on this uneasy-feeling bridge.

It's not specifically the bridge, I don't think it is; no, it's the exact spot I'm standing on which is particularly unnerving. The bridge itself didn't feel alien as I was walking back across, it's only this exact spot which is turning my brain to stars and my bowels to water. I have an overwhelming urge to sit down, right here on this peculiar and faintly burgundy stain, so I do, and then to lie down, which I also do, and tuck my knees into my chest, and close my eyes, and the bang-bang-bang of the nearby workmen with their hammers is more than I can take, and my eyelids flash with crimson light, and…

"Are you alright, sir?"

A policeman, pantomime white cuffs and all, standing above me.

"What? Yes, oh yes, completely fine officer, I, er, I was just…"

"Well perhaps you could get up sir, if you're able, this is a busy thoroughfare. Would you like some assistance?"

"No, no, I, no, thank you."

Well, that's a little embarrassing. A small crowd has gathered, no doubt hoping that I was dead or having some manner of entertaining seizure, because nothing amuses more than another's personal crises, and they look markedly disappointed as I stand up with relative ease and walk away without so much as a limp to satisfy their hunger for drama. Never mind, perhaps someone will get stabbed a little further up the bridge and give them all something to crow about.

I walk down the steps to the waterfront, and as I take a deep lungful of Thames air it occurs to me that this whole area would be markedly improved by the addition of a promenade, like the one on the north side of the river; the south bank offers equally beguiling views, and would surely benefit from somewhere to stroll and take in the sights, perhaps a few eateries and performing arts venues. I almost immediately regret breathing so deeply, as the air at this level is utterly foul, what seemed like sand from afar turning out to be a soup of mud and rotting quasi-organic matter, every step sucking in shoes and releasing noxious vapours. This river really is a sewer, a stew of foulness, there's no reason to be down here. What a revolting waterway this is.

Having climbed back up the stone steps in order to re-observe the river from above, it's remarkable how different it seems from up here. A broad, busy, impressive channel, pumping lifeblood in and out of the city. No sense of foulness here; indeed, it's almost majestic. I could stand here all day, staring across at the Houses of Parliament and chain-smoking my way through the contents of father's old silver cigarette case.

I wonder if he ever stared out over this view. Everybody should. It's the essence of London, distilled. And the river hardly stinks at all.

I arrive at Smith's (the café, not the office) fifteen minutes early and she's already there, arching an eyebrow at a newspaper and delicately sipping tea from a chipped china mug as if it were the finest porcelain. What an entirely fascinating creature.

There's no hello as I sit down opposite her at the small table, she simply launches straight into "My *magnum opus*, then, my so-called Hater's Head…"

"Ought we to order first?" I ask, although it isn't really a question.

"It's done," she says, with a tone implying that such fripperies are a poor use of her time. "I ordered us both the pie and mash, although inexplicably they have no liquor."

"No, it's not really that sort of place. I wouldn't expect the mash to be particularly mashed, and the pie may well be all crust."

"No matter. I was partway through my story, was I not?"

"Indeed you were. Please, continue."

"It began in France, you see," she says, finishing her tea and signalling for another, although I suspect the dispassionate staff of Smith's may not be *au fait* with such gestures. "Well, perhaps not 'began' as such. May I be candid with you, Mr...?"

"You may," I smile, dodging the identifier. My veil is my shield, it must never slip.

"I was at Roedean as a child, until an unfortunate letter arrived instructing me to return home forthwith. My father, mercurial character as he was, had gone bankrupt."

"I see."

"The humiliation was unbearable. He left us in penury, high-tailing it off alone to America to rebuild himself. He'd run a map publishing company before it somehow all came crashing down, and..."

"Aha, I can see where this is going."

"I'm sorry?"

"No, do go on."

She bristles. "So I was sent to France, forced to live hand-to-mouth as he'd left us with nothing. Desolate. Until, that was, I met Dick."

"Dick?"

"My husband. I had been visiting my brother, who was something of an artist, you see, living in Paris, and in his artistic Bohemian circles I met the charming and endearing Dick Pearsall, a man of whom I grew immediately fond. We married soon afterwards."

The mood has shifted somewhat. It feels as if all of her violets have wafted out of the café door and out into the filth of Covent Garden, their delicate aroma crushed by the city.

"We travelled, we painted, we nourished one another's souls across the length and breadth of Europe."

An artist with a penchant for travel and adventure with something to prove to her father, who has a history of map-related endeavours? "Yes, the pieces of the puzzle are starting to slot together, I see."

"But let's skip forward a few years. Having completed my London odyssey, I employed the services of one of my father's old cartographers, one who'd worked on his mapping of London before the Great War."

"Your husband did all of the walking with you, did he?"

"No, no, I left him behind in Venice years ago. As I was saying..."

"Hang on – you father produced a map of London before?"

"Yes."

"And you used the same cartographer to map out your own findings?"

"Yes."

"So isn't your map largely the same as your father's?"

"Sir, you forget that the city is expanding. Much has changed. The war reshaped the cityscape, industry booms, population magnifies."

"OK, OK. And... I'm sorry to keep going on about this, but you really walked every street to do this? Would it not have been rather simpler to visit each London County Council office and use their own maps to fuse together?"

"That, sir, is a suggestion so absurd as to not warrant a response."

"Oh. Fair enough."

"The fact of the matter is this: with demons exorcised and endeavours completed, the A-Z exists as a complete work in perfect-bound paper, ready for your perusal."

"Ah, I can see it?"

"But of course. Ten thousand copies are printed and ready for distribution. It is at this point that we arrive at the crux of my story."

She reaches into the leather shoulder bag hanging from the empty chair beside her and retrieves a pale yellow paperback, handing it to me with an expression of such devastating hopefulness that I wonder whether she realises that her mask has slipped.

The book is thick and substantial, with an imposing silhouette of Tower Bridge opening on the cover. *'Atlas and guide to London and suburbs, with house numbers,'* it promises. *'The only quick map reference supplement to all old and new street names'.*

"The distillation of a life's work," she breathes. And the meaning is clear. This isn't simply a year of walking, this is a second chance at a life derailed.

I flick through its crisp pages. There's a supreme privilege to being the first person to turn the leaves of a freshly printed book; how many other people will turn these very pages over the years? Will this one sit idle and unregarded on a shelf, or rest well-thumbed on the coffee table? Will it survive the generations or be callously discarded after a matter of months? Will it be treated gently, or have its spine cracked and its margins scribbled? A new book is like a newborn baby, the possibilities are entirely limitless. Fresh stories to be written and rewritten every day.

"So… can you help me?" she asks, almost imperceptibly, words that are more felt within the soul than heard through the ears.

"How do you mean?"

"You know, at WHSmith's. I need distribution. These books need to sell. Do you make decisions? Or can you show this to the people who do?"

I smile at her, without mirth or amusement but simply pleasant civility, and against any sense of better judgment, offer a little nod.

Her face melts into happiness, transforming the room as the air appears to glow around her, the violets returning with glorious warmth.

And here I am, callously getting her hopes up with an empty smile.

Chapter Fourteen

On the uncivil side of 6am, as the sun's just negotiating with the horizon to determine whether or not it fancies actually getting up at all, rural France may as well be on a different planet to suburban Britain. Above you only sky; no planes, no squawking gulls, no helicopters, no edgy tension of the air being imminently rent by sirens. The air itself feels crisper, more spaced apart, not cloying at all. You shimmer through the ozone with icy lungfuls, it feels so clean.

I ease open the front door, decades-old muscle memory ensuring that by slightly lifting it as I turn, and tilting it a little toward its hinges, its trademark creak doesn't sound. Tricks of the teens, they never leave you. Sneaking out of places is one of the staples of existence, honed in video games and then made deliciously tangible by the necessity to shimmer out to the pub. I tiptoe down the stairs to the garage, its doors pleasingly only held closed with the little exterior hook rather than the myriad bolts affixed to the other side, because this isn't the sort of place where people just wander into each other's garages, never has been, the locks are just for the insurance man. And there it is, just as I was hoping it would still be, dad's old Renault 4, resplendent in faded-to-matt beige and rusty dings and crumbling window rubbers, purchased to allow us to slip about the countryside incognito rather than being segregated with the oft-loathed Brits Abroad. His straw hat is absent from the parcel shelf, as is mum's, and this is momentarily so crushing that I just want to dissolve to the ground and weep at the incompleteness of the memory, so near and yet so far, but wait, no, they're hanging on pegs on the wall next to the key box. The key box which is also unlocked. Oh, France. You're decades out of step.

Has Madame Aznavour been keeping the car in good order too? Seems like a level outside of her remit, whatever that might specifically be, and yet there's air in the tyres and fuel in the tank, so I reckon there's a strong chance of success here. These things just go on forever, don't they? They don't break, they're hardy and rustic, like the farmers who own them. They just don't die.

And here it goes. As sure as the tides, as sure as the sun, the starter spins for a few seconds and the puttering little motor catches, a puff of gentle smoke from the rear, ready to go, terrier-like, as it ever was. I chug backwards out of the narrow garage, the accelerator's much lighter than in that massive BMW, I'm accidentally revving the engine way too high and it sounds like a swarm of wasps inside a coffee can, and the wing mirror scrapes reassuringly along the groove in the garage door where it's scraped a thousand times before, and the clutch is lighter too and the car jerks backwards as I fully release it and one of the wheels skips over a rock, jinking the car slightly sideways, and I whirl the steering wheel in the other direction and the back of the Renault smacks noisily into the front corner of the BMW, taillight and headlight colourfully merging as one and tinkling down into the gravel. Bollocks.

"That's quite a show you're putting on," says Wilson, looking down from the top of the steps as I scrabble about on hands and knees to assess the damage.

Shit. I was never allowed to drive the car, even though all the kids around here are bouncing 2CVs across fields from the age of ten, legality be damned, I'd always wanted to drive the thing and was always rebuffed, and here I am bumping it on my first try. And he saw. For fuck's sake. But he's smiling, so that's OK, but is it OK, god, why does he always smile at my misfortune?

"I, er… I wasn't running away, officer," I say, and I'm not entirely sure why.

"I didn't say you were."

"No, I mean, I know it must look odd, me driving off at the crack of dawn and leaving you here alone, but I just, I don't want to miss it."

"Miss what?"

"The sunrise. It looks amazing from the top of the hill. Do you want to see?"

"Do I have time to put some clothes on?"

I thought he *was* wearing clothes. They're very formal pyjamas, I wonder where one would acquire such a set of garments. I didn't know grown-ups even wore pyjamas. If I'd been woken up by some ham-fisted cretin crashing cars about at stupid o'clock, I'd have been rushing out in my pants. Thank goodness he's more mature than I am.

"Um… if you're quick. I'll, er, I'll manoeuvre my way out of this, you go and throw a shirt on."

He pops back into the house and I restart the Renault, engaging first and pulling forward, realising the steering's still on full lock and I'm heading back into the garage, sticking it in reverse, and backing straight into the fucking BMW again, for fuck's sake, then forward at a slightly different angle toward the corner of the house, then arcing round gracefully and crashing ever-so-gently into the BMW's door, Christ, and continuing to drive like an absolute piece until eventually I'm facing in the right direction and Wilson's standing there, fully clothed, bent double with laughter, tears streaming from his eyes.

"Get in. Just shut up and get in."

We trundle up the lane, mercifully managing not to fucking crash into anything because I don't think he'd ever let me hear the end of it, but it's fine, I mean at least he's seeing a funny side, if I were him I'd be refusing to get in the car with someone so clearly bloody inept, it's OK, it's OK, and we creak and crunch down to the part where the road narrows as the trees form a tunnel above it, so narrow that dad once forgot which side of the road to drive on when he was startled by an oncoming Mini and reflexively swerved to the left, straight towards it, forcing it into the ditch, and he simply carried on and remarked upon how few Minis you see in France, and half a mile later as the tunnel broadens out we're driving up, up, steeply into the sky, improbably steeply, the plucky Renault scrabbling like a mountain goat, until after a herculean effort that further enrages the wasps in the coffee can we're on the level at the summit, a grassy bald with a bench among the wildflowers. We're just in time.

Wilson sits next to me on the bench, and I idly wish that I'd got up slightly earlier to make a flask of coffee. I may or may not have voiced this out loud, as he wordlessly reaches into his inside pocket and retrieves a hip flask, taking a quick nip and passing it to me. Smoky harshness rips across my throat, and I'm immediately impressed by this wholly unpolicelike behaviour. I thought coppers only misbehaved like that in books.

"Jesus, what is *that*?"

"Laphroaig," he says. "I hope you don't mind, I filled it up from your cocktail cabinet."

"No, no, not at all. Breakfast of champions."

The milky orange light is starting to bleed gloriously over the horizon, and you can see so far from here, all the way to the Massif Central, and there's a vee of geese flying above the woodland we've just puttered through, and wisps of dew burning off the fields miles away where the sun's already hit, and we sit and we wait. Just like mum and dad and I used to sit here waiting, just waiting, for the sunlight to bathe us in the freshness of a new day; every dawn a rebirth.

A pinprick, jarring in its violence among the serenity of the scene, jabs into my ankle, and it's a fucking wasp, what's a wasp doing up at this time of day anyway, little bastard, they're lazy little shits, they don't even make honey or do anything useful, they just fly about the place making people's days worse, and it's entangled in my trouser leg and stings me again as I slap at it, fucker, and that really has killed the mood of my whimsical reminiscing, I'd been so relaxed. Bloody hell, I'd forgotten how much wasp stings sting, I mean the clue's in the name but really, little bastard, but calm down, it's fine, remember years ago at the work summer party when that bee stung you on the hand? That really hurt. This isn't as bad as that. Nowhere near.

Still though, at least bees have the decency to die after they sting you.

I shake out my trouser leg, and the twitching little shithouse tumbles down into the grass. I take great pleasure in grinding his crunchy little body into the dirt with my heel. I'm not a cruel person by nature, when I find a spider in the house I'll cup it in my hands and deliver it to the garden, I shoo flies out of the window rather than squishing them with a rolled-up newspaper, but wasps really can sod off.

Wilson folds up his handkerchief, holds it over the hip flask and gives it a little shake, wordlessly dabbing the whisky onto my stings, and I wonder if I should point out that that's exactly what dad would have done, but this whole wasp episode has passed satisfyingly wordlessly and I'm enjoying the cinematic balance of that and I don't want to taint the mood, so I simply offer him a slight nod, like De Niro would, then sit back down beside him. The sunlight is just reaching us by this point, its warmth caressing the reset button, and again our lives begin anew.

The further we drive, the more I'm warming to the Renault, it just feels so appropriate to the scene, not like that absurd BMW, that doesn't fit in here at all, too brash, too modern. There's a simplicity to this, just an arrangement of plastic rectangles in front of me with a single dial; if I were to stretch out my arms I could probably hold onto both sides of the car if I so wished, although Wilson would possibly be a little alarmed at my suddenly relinquishing control of the wheel. An unexpected dual carriageway speeds the journey down to Pampelonne, I don't remember it being there so it must be new, but that's progress for you. I mean, all roads in France look new all the time, they resurface them a lot, not like in England where it seems to be a national sport to collect potholes, but what turns out to be the N88 is glassy-smooth. Although, given the rustic nature of this utilitarian old battle wagon, I think I'd prefer a rutted track or some bumpy grass. Isn't that what these things were designed for?

I reach under the dash to find the stereo dad had wired in there, hidden from view, and my fingers remember exactly where the on-off button is, and glory be, it works. A Graham Parker cassette, of course, how could it be anything else, playing *First Day of Spring* as if no other song in the world should exist at this particular moment.

"Do you mind if I ask where we're going?" says Wilson, and it's a fair question, I'm in my own little world really. Now I think about it, it's impressive that he didn't pipe up when we drove straight past the house and carried on going through the town and out the other side, out into the hills. That was a good twenty minutes ago, we're nearly at Tanus now.

I shrug. "Does it matter?"

"I suppose not."

I rub my eyes, suddenly aware that I'm exhausted. It doesn't feel like the exhaustion of a hangover, or the exhaustion of a lack of sleep; more like the culmination of an over-lived life. My soul, it needs to rest. "We're going to look at a bridge."

He doesn't question this, merely takes another nip of whisky, hands me the flask, and continues staring contentedly at the fields rolling by, their haybales like absurd brown cotton-reels in the sun.

The tape's turned itself over as we enter Pampelonne, god, remember how impressive auto-reverse used to feel back when it was new, how innovative, and dad's recorded Terrorvision on the other side, that's a bit of a contrast, and maybe I actually recorded this tape, it's a distinct possibility. The rickety slide in the playground in the square looks precisely as rickety as ever it did, on the verge of collapse but clearly having found its niche in the balance of the cosmos, frozen haphazardly in time, and we turn right, past the church, past the pharmacy, down to the edge of town, as Tony Wright asks *Alice, what's the matter?*, and snake balletically down the hairpins, past the ruined castle with its perilously deep craters that used to terrify me so wonderfully, at once safe and on the edge of death, down and down the extravagantly hairpinned road to the bridge over the Viaur. I pull into the gravelled clearing at the near side of the bridge and shut the Renault off, wondering as I climb out if I could get away with giving it a gentle pat, good car, well done, but that might look a little bit mental.

"This is it," I say, with unnecessary grandeur, and for a moment I feel crushingly awkward for driving half-an-hour here to show him what is actually quite an unimpressive bridge. I mean, it impresses me, it's tall and solid and stony, but it's the memories attached to it that help it grow in stature for me, and I'm achingly aware that to a new pair of eyes this might just appear to be yet another not-very-impressive bridge, probably not even the best one we've seen this morning.

"It's beautiful," he says, casually ambling down the centre of the road, and the relief is so devastatingly huge that my legs are momentarily weakened, I have to lean against the stone wall to regain composure.

"Yeah. It's alright, isn't it?"

It's too early for the campers to be splashing about, although the smell of enthusiastically cremating meat indicates that there's activity down on the site, and the river is as yet empty of canoes and pedalos; all there is down there is the gentle slop-slap of water against the base of the bridge, and shoals of silvery fish darting about the place like nothing matters. The heat of the morning sun has already softened the tarmac over the bridge, and I could weep with the joy of seeing how my trainers have left a perfect sole imprint in a soft patch at the edge of the road. It's all I can do to stop myself getting down on my knees, grabbing a twig, and signing my handiwork in the gooey tarmac. And then I figure what the hell, here's a man who's travelled seven-hundred miles to find me and is still yet to really explain

why that is, and has instead opted to have whisky for breakfast, and he's hardly in any position to judge, so sod it, I'm doing it. I kneel down, gravel poking into my kneecaps, sharp and painful and yet beautiful as it's such a child-like feeling, it feels so fresh, and I start to carve my first initial into the road beside my footprint, and suddenly there's a horn blaring, a Focus, an old one, in a sort of watery shade of green, careening out of control across the bridge, come in too fast, not slowed down enough coming down the hill, I can smell its hot brakes, and here I am kneeling down like an idiot, and Wilson grabs me by the arm and yanks me to one side of the road as the car swerves to the other, scraping and crunching along the low stone wall, shards of headlight glass tinkling to the ground, and the driver recovers and he's over the bridge and away, lurching left into the forest road, and I listen to his rasping exhaust echoing through the trees until it's completely faded and serenity returns.
"Fucking hell," says Wilson, and I can't help but agree.

Sometimes I just yearn for finality, it can become too much to bear. A bolt from the blue, that's the way to go, none of this agonising over the moral implications of seeking an exit, simply having the decision-making process beautifully removed from your scope, allowing you the freedom to disappear without a word. When I was a kid, I had a page sellotaped to my bedroom wall that I'd torn out of a science book in the school library, about a place called Manson in Iowa. In general Iowa is pretty flat, this extract explained, but in the 1950s they discovered that underneath the topsoil was a crater three miles deep and twenty miles across. There's only one thing that can make a hole that big, and that's a fucking great asteroid. Sudden chaotic destruction from above, and not a damn thing you can do about it. The concept of that really struck a chord with me – no matter how hard you try, how eager you are to please, how much effort you put into planning for your future, everything could be erased at a moment's notice with no warning. It makes life a little less intimidating, doesn't it? Apparently there's over a billion of these asteroids whizzing about up there, and quite a few of them are big enough to imperil civilisation; even more exciting is that there are two or three near-misses with asteroids of this scale every week. Any one of these, if they were to hit us, would probably wipe out humanity in one fell swoop. No warning, no escape. How would it kill us? Well, the asteroid itself would vaporise before technically making impact, but the compressed air between it and the Earth's surface – picture a rock five miles across travelling hundreds of times faster than a bullet – would heat to something like ten times the temperature of the surface of the sun, as compressed air heats very effectively, meaning that everything in its path would also vaporise. Every living thing for hundreds of miles around that hadn't been killed by the heat would be crushed by the thousands of tons of superheated rock that would blast out of the crater. Within minutes, the ensuing shockwave would flatten everything for thousands of miles. Next would come a global chain of earthquakes, volcanoes and tsunamis, clouds of burning rock would pelt every metre of the planet's surface, setting the world on fire, and ionic disturbances would knock out all means of communication, so even if there was a safe place to run to, which there wouldn't be, you'd have no way of knowing. The ash cloud would blot out the sun for years, meaning that anyone who was lucky enough to survive would soon die of starvation or malnutrition. It was an idea I was obsessed with, and right now, right here, on this bridge, just like on the other bridge, it feels deliciously tangible. This could happen *at any moment*. Sure, it might not happen for hundreds of thousands of years, but it could happen today, right now. Impacts on the scale of Manson happen, on average, about once every million years. And that one occurred 2.5 million years ago. C'mon, cosmos, show me what you've got. You keep taking these fucking shots at me, let's see something *really* impressive.

I don't have it in me to protest as Wilson offers to drive back to the house, and his tone suggests that it's really more of a demand than an offer anyway. Fine by me. I lie down in the back seat, as much as is possible at least, and swill back what remains in the hip flask. This is pleasingly out of kilter with what being in the back of this car should be like; as a teenager, sitting back here meant either that we were on the way to buy something or to eat something. Shopping for groceries or DIY paraphernalia to do to the house whatever the parental whims had decided over last night's wine, or off somewhere for dinner; a restaurant, which was OK, or a farmhouse, which was better. Farmers always have the most interestingly stocked wine cellars and cocktail cabinets. And they each have their signature eau de vie, each more potent and probably toxic than the last. I remember one time, the farmer from a couple of villages over, I couldn't tell you where, the memories of that night were smashed to pieces, he brought out the absinthe after dinner. And this wasn't your wishy-washy store-bought absinthe, this was the pukka wormwood shit, immediately rewiring your brain and fucking with your perceptions, poured over a sugar cube and straight into your soul. I didn't get any sleep that night, I couldn't, my brain wouldn't let me, so I read an *Asterix* book, and all the characters were marching out of the pages and walking around the room, Obelix munching on wild boar and Dogmatix yapping about the place, and it was too freaky to deal with so I went out to the living room and there was dad sitting in the armchair, in the dark, hands gripping the armrests so tight his knuckles were white, wide-eyed like a lunatic staring straight through time, he must have been there for hours. Ah, they were the days.

But sitting back here, being chauffeured around the countryside by an unexplained policeman, I'm neither going to shop nor going to eat. I'm simply going. Going somewhere. Going home? Most likely, but to be honest it really doesn't matter. I could not care less.

Cooking chicken on the barbecue requires a specific knack that I've never been able to master. No matter how much you move it around, or how frequently you turn it, the flesh always welds itself to the grill in some way, meaning that the tines, are they tines, or is that forks I'm thinking of, whatever, the tines always get caked in blackened and charred bits of chicken so no matter how good the cooked product may ultimately be, there's always the certainty of a difficult scrubbing session when you've finished, every second of cooking further galvanising the escaped meat fragments, making poultry and steel fuse as one, so Wilson better bloody appreciate me cooking chicken for him, because frankly the stress is more than I can bear. But it's fine, relax, keep calm, there's always the sausages. The French really know their way around a sausage, there's no denying that. Nice big curl of Toulouse sausage, satisfyingly meaty in its chunkiness, skewered right through and cooked as one like some macabre Hallowe'en Danish pastry.

"So, Brian," I say, casually, incredibly proud of myself that I've actually used his first name and hoping like hell that he won't register the gravity of the achievement and will simply let the conversation flow naturally as it should between two adults, "tell me again how you knew my mother."

I've used the word 'again' because it sounds relaxed and comfortable, like we've already discussed it at length and I'm just making idle chit-chat with another man through barbecue smoke, which is a gruff and outdoorsy endeavour. We are men, we make fire. Wilson's been buggering about with prawns, big fat juicy kings, skewering them, punctuating them on the rods with quarter-slices of chorizo and hunks of green pepper, and he'd better not upstage me with those because they look bloody delicious and I want my sausage to be the focal point here, I mean shit, not like that, but honestly, seafood? Strong addition to the barbecue oeuvre but it shouldn't be the talking point. And fuck it all, there's going to be none of this chicken left if it all keeps gluing itself to fucking grill, seriously, come on. But it's fine, take another slug of whisky, that seems to be the way the day's going, you're alright, you're alright.

"Well… there's not much to tell," he says, which is just the most annoying answer imaginable. But no, give him a chance, come on. "I told you how I met her, she helped me…"

"…stitch up your savaged ballbag, yes. That must have been agonising." Don't ask to see it, don't ask to see it, you don't want to see it, it's just your brain defaulting to that frightening position where it suggests you do the most humiliatingly out-of-context thing possible just to mess with you, the way it tells you to kiss the plumber after he's fixed your boiler or cup the breast of the lady in the Post Office after she's sold you a book of stamps, stupid brain, just fuck off, I really should stop drinking, it's still only midday.

"It did smart a bit, yes." He takes a deep pull from a Leffe, god, who even drinks that, and I can't think of anything I'd like more in the world, I'll go to the fridge and get one when this chicken's finished cremating itself. "She stitched me up and sent me on my way, told me to come back the next day for a fresh dressing."

"Uh-huh."

"And so I went back the next day. For a fresh dressing."

"Uh-huh. Do you…?" I point at his beer and do the shaky-hand international symbol for 'another beer', which I suspect as soon as I start shaking my hand that I might actually have just made up, but he seems to get it and he nods, and I dart inside and grab a couple of those strong sweaty brews from the fridge, darting right back out again just in time to see the fucking chicken going fully up in flames, for *fuck*'s sake.

"That, er… that wasn't the last she saw of me. I mean, that I saw of her."

Woah. Steady, Brian. "No?" I ask, slightly too airily.

"No, she asked me if I'd like to go to the pictures with her."

Bloody hell, 'to the pictures'. When was this, bloody 1954?

"Ha, that must be some mighty impressive scrotum you've got there."

Christ, why did I say that? That has to be absolutely the worst thing I've ever said to anybody, what an appallingly crass thing to say, but wow, he's blushing, I've never seen him blush, there's a *human* in there, and he's also slightly grinning, and I'm not entirely sure what to make of this. But my sausage appears to be ready, shit, I hope there's no symbolism in that, which is a marvellous piece of timing because suddenly it feels rather difficult to stand up. I slap my meat onto a plate, ha, and flop into a folding chair, while he takes my place at the grill and delicately lines up his prawn skewers, perfect spacing between them, and he has the decency not to mention the jagged mounds of ex-chicken blackening the things, they're not tines, what are they? Doesn't matter. Man, this beer goes down easy. Ooh, and he's put a few more in an ice bucket under the table, when did he do that, stout fellow, tip-top.

"We didn't become an item or anything like that, but we did go on a couple of dates. She… she seemed to understand me. I mean, she had a warmth, an easy kinship, she could empathise very easily with you. A good listener."

Oh god, she really was a good listener. "Yes, I think that's the thing I miss the most. The listening. I mean, not that I've got a huge amount to say, I'm not really a talker, most of my talking really happens inside my head but I have the sense not to let it out, you know, you learn to shut up when you realise no-one wants to hear it, but mum, she knew, you know, she understood.

I could say anything to her."

"And who do you talk to now?"

Interesting. A point it had never occurred to me to consider.

I polish off another beer, genuinely impressed by how each one is easing the passage for its peers, paving the way for the next, I may never stand again. "You, I guess."

The shifting light takes on an entirely different character as the sun goes down. In the daytime, the sunlight refracts through the opaque plastic pyramid over the swimming pool and illuminates the cavity of air above the surface with a uniform brightness, mimicking the glare of the sunlight outside, but the character of the pool fractures and transmogrifies as the sun begins to go down, the underwater lights flicking on automatically and illuminating the rippling surface from below; the dynamic is shifted, with the brightness beaming from beneath and the air above taking on a milky orange quality that recalls the fledgling sunlight that pours over the hills at dawn. Every diverse and disparate element of the natural beauty of the countryside is represented within this capsule, an aquatic microcosm as much as it is an exceptional hiding place.

The reality of coming to terms with the fact that you're more alone than you think you are is a distasteful and unnerving one, and when Wilson nips off to the loo I scamper down the back stairs, across the lawn, which Madame Aznavour really has been doing a sterling job of maintaining, I don't ever remember it being this perfect under dad's care, it's like a putting green from a video game, and slide up the huge square of Perspex that serves as an entrance to the pool. I remember dad being furious at the necessity of that, apoplectic, after the endless months of digging out the massive hole in the ground, hiring in locals with mini-diggers to haul the thick claggy soil out of the pit, then finishing it off by hand with a spade, back-breaking, when he ran out of money to pay them; then there was the pouring of the concrete, and smashing it all out to start again when the mixture went to cock, followed by the spiralling time-suck of applying every single one of those baby-blue tiles by hand, week after inexorable week, and the oh-so-careful borders planted around the edges of the pool to frame it as some sort of garden art piece.

Looking out from an upstairs window, it looked like a glorious framed picture laid out on the lawn. And then the inspector came by and said that legally it either needed to have a tall fence around it or an all-enclosing structure, for safety, monsieur, so that children and animals can't fall into it, and it took a remarkable amount of eau de vie to talk the inspector down from the litigious ledge having found out that there was no planning permission, and eventually the compromise was reached to engineer this vast Perspex pyramid.

But mum pointed out that it looked like the entrance to the Louvre, and everything was OK again. She had a gift for steering him away from fury and back into cheerfulness. I wonder at which point that gift escaped her. No, no, it wasn't *her* fault, it was something in him that made it all go sour.

And so, clothes discarded aside from my boxers, no time to grab trunks, I just have to be alone, I slip into the entrance of the Louvre and down into the warm water. The sunset at the end of the pool is represented by a searing yet distorted disc of orange, dazzling and at the same time hugely comforting, as the citrus rays play about the surface of the water, mingling with the light shining from beneath.

I hold onto the edge, gripping slightly too tightly, steeling myself, eager to see if I can still do it after all these years, and plunge below the water line, eyes screwed up tight and kicking furiously, arms sweeping in great arcs, this feels like I must be at least halfway, must be, and how many more strokes will it be, perhaps this isn't possible after all, Jesus, my lungs can't cope with this, it's too far, but I can't be that far away from the end of the pool, just a couple more strokes, no, fuck it, my lungs are going to implode, I can see sparkles dancing inside my eyelids, no, I have to surface, I have to breathe, I can't do this, I don't know why I ever try to achieve anything, useless boy, futile, and there it is, my fingertips touching the edge of the pool, I've done it, I've made the full length, and I surface in a fit of gasps and choking.

The agony of it feels so good. I have to do it again. Two deep breaths and I'm under, surging through the water, the lights beaming brightly through my tight-shut eyelids, ears ringing, muscles burning, and *fuck it all* it's even harder this time, I can't even be halfway, keep kicking, keep fucking kicking you useless little turd, this is why you're alone, you always fucking give up on things, letting life walk all over you, no, come on, you have to give up now, it's going to kill you, do what you always do, fail, give up, and there it is, the far fucking wall scratching beautifully at my skin, and I surface choking once more.

Wilson's sitting on the steps, wiggling his toes in the water and seemingly entirely unfazed. God, I didn't want to be alone, I just wanted to fucking achieve something, and it's hard to tell whether it's a warm wave of familiarity that I'm feeling or simply an actual warm wave. My heart's beating so hard it feels like it's going to hammer through my ribcage altogether and leave me to bob about without it, my leg muscles are burning, my arms so overworked they're shaking uncontrollably, and I'm acutely aware of the wasp stings, the treatments in the water tickling and playing with them for their own chemical amusement. Devastatingly I feel completely sober, and that comes as a colossal insult, there is no greater disappointment than sobriety, but Wilson, wonderful Wilson, has brought a couple of beers in with him, and the decadence of drinking strong beer while floating in a swimming pool as the sun goes down is enough to click my reset button with extraordinary satisfaction. The emotional yo-yo once again spools itself back into neatness. Everything is right with the world. Everything is fine.

"It wouldn't have worked out between us," Wilson says, towelling his hair, as I carefully install mum's urn back to its rightful place in the centre of the mantelpiece, commanding the room as she should, god she could command a room.

"What, you and me? What do you...?"

"Yeah, that's right, me and you." He rolls his eyes theatrically, I mean, it seems theatrical, when's the last time I went to the theatre? No idea. Decades. "No, between me and your mum, you div."

Ah, 'div'. A beautiful relic from a time forgotten. Right up there with 'spanner' and 'prat'. I'm glad we've moved on from the 'sir'/'officer' dynamic, the casual abuse feels far more comfortable.

"She was wonderful company, but I was just taking too much from her and not giving anything back. It's the nature of my work, you see, you don't... you don't get to *express* yourself very much. I was just haemorrhaging emotion toward her and she was soaking it up like, er, you know, like a tortured nursing simile. Cigar?"

"I'm sorry?"

"Would you like a cigar?"

He does love to blindside you with an unexpected question.

"Sure, why not?"

I've always been crap at smoking cigars. The whole process feels counterintuitive, the point of smoking is to take it down into your lungs, right, that's what you do with ciggies and joints, it's just natural, it's breathing with extras, but with a cigar you have to make a conscious effort not to inhale it, so you end up ballooning your cheeks like a hamster and going slightly red and wide-eyed, and then puffing out a thick cloud of white smoke and rapidly inhaling fresh air like someone who's just emerged from swimming a length of the pool underwater because you suddenly realise you haven't been breathing for about thirty seconds, and I really hope he doesn't judge me too harshly for not smoking his cigar properly, although by this stage of the day I feel we're comfortable enough in one another's company for it not to matter too much.

He lights it for me, a Guantanamera about the size of hot dog that's had its top-third chomped off, and immediately the house smells like it did back in the early nineties. I had no idea that dad used to smoke cigars, I never saw him do it, but this smell, this is exactly what the house smelled of when I got up in the mornings, I'd always just assumed it was the woodsmoke from the fire. Why didn't it ever occur to me that we didn't often light the fire in summer, when even in the evenings it was still thirty degrees outside, and considerably warmer in here with these two-foot-thick walls? The pieces of my naivety continue to slot into place.

"So I told her I had to leave," he continues, as I deal out a hand of rummy on the dining table, giving him the extra card, delighted to find that I'm holding a pair of sevens and a run of clubs so I only have a couple more cards to find. "It wasn't a big deal, or at least it didn't seem so at the time, we'd only been on a couple of dates. I told her I had to travel to another part of the country for work, and that I'd see her again at some indeterminate point in the future, and that point never arrived. In hindsight, though..."

"Yes?" Awesome, I've picked up another seven. In your face, fate.

He studies his cards with measured consideration. "In hindsight, there may well have been more to it than I realised. She certainly stayed in my thoughts for years afterwards." He glances up toward the urn, just a flicker, the briefest glimmer, but it's everything, that split-second glance, dripping in pathos. "Seeing her photo framed in your house, it felt like a homecoming. Like I'd returned to the place I should always have been. Is that… is that an odd thing to say?"

I honestly can't think of an answer to that. I mean, she is, she was, my mother, *mine*, and who was this strange character from the past anyway, how can he suddenly have such apparent significance in the wake of all the strangeness that's happened of late?

I take a fresh card, but I don't look at it just yet. I can't help but study his face, searching for clues, any sort of clues, although god only knows what I'm expecting to find.

It's a two, a throwaway two. Two is no good to me.

"And I can assure you that she only saw my scrotum on a strictly medical basis," he says, slapping down three kings and four twos. Bastard.

We've moved onto the wine by the time the evening enters the VHS zone, movement of any kind feeling increasingly unnecessary save for sporadic trips to the lavatory or to top up the crisp bowls. France has come on in leaps and bounds in the crisp game, it's really quite impressive. Back in the nineties, your options were pretty much limited to ready salted or, you know, ready salted, but one day clearly an executive from Stoc or Intermarché went on a day trip to Dover and came back with the astounded proclamation that, *sacré bleu*, their crisps taste of things over there. And there was an overnight paprika explosion, and suddenly the crisp aisles in the shops quadrupled in size. It's quite a shock if you're not expecting it, I can tell you.

We'd eased out another Cuvée Prestige, a 1991 this time, because I'd found mum and dad's old notebook from the Gaillac wine festival and the notes, spidery in their gorgeously drunken scrawl, suggested that this was some seriously good shit (unlike

the 'pigswill' at the next stand; drunken honesty is entirely
without filter), and I ham-fistedly jab a corkscrew into the top as
Wilson scrabbles about on hands and knees fiddling with the
VCR. Inevitably the aged cork snaps in half, I hate it when they
do that, can't help but take it personally, but I know that the
tactic here is to v-e-r-y carefully thread the end of the corkscrew
into what remains of the brittle cork halfway down the neck, so
this is what I attempt, and immediately manage to inadvertently
shove the remainder of the cork right down into the bottle, *fuck it
all*, but that's fine because the wine can at least pour out around
the remnants so all is not lost, and I attempt to decant the
Prestige into a glass but the half-cork floats into the way and acts
as a stopper, and as I jiggle the bottle to dislodge it, the cork
moves very quickly aside and I pour almost all of the bottle over
the table, dropping and smashing it in the process and briefly
yearning just for a moment to be literally anywhere else in the
world. But my brain reminds me that somewhere out in the
wider world is a Jed with a large knife, and suddenly my
slapstick endeavours feel pretty comfortable. Sod it.
Continuing the theme of our developing acquaintance, I once
again find that Wilson is creased up with laughter at my
misfortune, but by this stage I really couldn't care less. The cork
comes out of the next bottle rather more easily, almost
serendipitously in fact, and a cynic might suggest that this is
because Wilson is doing the uncorking instead of me but I've got
no time for cynics. All about positivity, me. So I have decent red
wine and crisps that taste of things and there's a suave Space
Corps test pilot dimension-jumping on TV and everything is
alright in the world. I ease back into the armchair, not dad's
armchair, the other armchair, Wilson has assumed the dad role,
in armchair terms I mean, and wow this room feels warm.
Overly warm. Weirdly warm? I can see that Wilson feels it too,
and he stands and walks toward the mantel, and I stand and do
the same, and the heat radiating from the urn is really quite
intense, and we both place a palm on its smooth and slightly
textured sides and just stand and absorb its energy.
And then we sit again, glasses brimmed, and it's cold outside
and there's no kind of atmosphere, and the wine is creating its
own warmth inside of us, and my eyelids are heavy, it's not just
tiredness, it's an exhaustion of the soul, a necessity for
everything to just stop, enough, stop now, and Wilson's eyes are

closing too, I can see the heaviness in him, and I recline and let sleep take me, the wine glass tumbling to the floor and who cares, that's a problem for another time.

Chapter Fifteen

If there's one thing that would stop me from wanting to work in a hospital, aside from the gore and the tragedy and of course my own total absence of qualifications, it's the incessant beeping. Every room contains machines which beep and bloop and bleep and they're all doing vital and important jobs, and those beeps are reassuring to those who are expecting a constant staccato punctuation of beeps and are terrified of any sort of deviation from it, but man it gets inside your head. And there's enough inside my head already, thank you.

She doesn't seem to notice it though, she simply shimmers effortlessly from room to room, mopping a brow here, ticking a box on a flipchart there, a friendly smile for one and all, radiating warmth from every pore.

"Hi Viv," says Wilson as she passes, swirling violets with every step.

"Brian, hello," she smiles, utterly unfazed. "Shall we catch up later? It's mayhem in here."

And all of this feels perfectly natural, her calmness within the mayhem, the easy familiarity, and everyone expecting everyone else to be exactly where they are and it isn't strange at all. Wilson pushes a curtain aside and we see her, Céline Louvois, I thought she'd died on the bridge but no, here she is under the loving care of the busy stream of doctors and nurses, smiling through her respirator, sunlight gleaming out of every perfect bullethole. James Keyes in the next bed, a large part of his skull missing, pink, pulpy matter exposed to the violet scents of the ward, and yet also smiling, gleeful in the comfort of the surroundings, the beeps fading into a low level of background noise; Barrie Abeyour across the way, multiple punctures through the torso but revelling in the splendour of being in traction, at once so jarring and so comfortable. Pictures of mothers on bedside tables, fathers sitting beside patients and weeping, no, not weeping, oozing joy from their tear ducts, celebrating the majesty of the new dawn and everything the fresh rebirth brings with it. Everything here is shiny and new. Wilson sits beside a bed, and I cannot see the patient's face, the mask is as translucent as all the others but somehow the face is blurred, indistinct, and Wilson's face is in his hands and he's shuddering with the emotion, the intensity, and is he the only sad person in the room, it's really hard to say, but no, he's laughing, uproariously laughing, and the other dads are up and joining him, slapping each other on the back and raising the levels of sheer unfettered joy to stratospheric heights. And her hand is on my shoulder, ushering me out of the room, gently but firmly, and I take one final glance back to see the face but it's still so fuzzy and indistinct, and I'm in the corridor and she's sitting me down, and "Just wait here son, I'll be back soon," and I'm alone.

The peeling lino at the base of the bench is as familiar as that light fitting in my old bedroom, a gouged and dilapidated detail among the healing and rejuvenation that the building thrives upon. Minutes bleeding into hours, bleeding into days, perennially bleeding, staring down at that curling linoleum and waiting to be allowed in to see her, to see how she was doing on what they refuse to call her deathbed, every minute torture, every hour another pointless victory, every visit at once drawing me closer to her suffering and pushing me further, further from the normality. You can never go home again, not really, because what you know as 'home' is lying there in that bed, and when she goes she'll be taking such a large part of you with her that nothing will ever be truly homely again.
Beep.
Beep.
Beep.
Beeeeeeeeeeeeep.
The final beep, the one that I can't even allow myself to visualise, extended so sarcastically as a marker of finality, *'listen to me, doctors, this is the beepingest beep I can muster'*, a sound that will forever and always symbolise the end of everything that was pure and good, and it goes on for long enough that any sane person would be begging for the machine to be switched off, and even when the sound is extinguished it's still there in my head, *in my fucking head*, beeping relentlessly for all eternity. Will there ever be any peace? It's just an endless vista of beeping, a violent tinnitus, stretching off to the edge of the universe, and I'm tumbling through the door with the doctors and the nurses and the crash cart and it's too late, everyone in the room already

knows it's too late, it's over, and there's frantic activity and yet at the same time everything stops, and I'm curled up in a ball at the end of her bed and it's the last time I'll ever be able to be like this with her, and if I climb right under her bed one last time will the world just go away?

...the results returned to us from the technical inspection leave us in no doubt that the failure of the crash protection barrier was caused by the corrosion of the retaining bolts, their structural integrity weakened by the heightened levels of sodium chloride and potassium chloride in the ambient atmosphere. While extensive crash-testing was carried out prior to installation, the absence of regular pressure testing and/or integrity maintenance resulted in an inevitable shearing of bolts when subjected to the pressure of the moving vehicle. In addition, whereas regular traffic collision modelling would foresee a potential impact as an immediate but ultimately brief event, the notion of a sustained and deliberate impact along a greater length of barrier was not factored into the structural equation. As such, the barrier was unable to fulfil its required task of separating pavement and road and the perimeter was quickly breached...

The eddies of the breeze are surprisingly warm up here, looping around the Eye, across the Thames and through the monumental scaffolding of the clock tower, along the north bank to the dome of St Paul's, swirling down to rustle leaves over *The Tempest*, not cool as you'd imagine but creamy-warm like a cuddle. We hold hands as we hover way, way above the grey-brown murk of the river, gently buffeted by those gorgeous smatterings of breezes, oh, *your life, ooh, it may be a dream.*

The little green car looks almost cartoonishly cute from above, trundling up from the IMAX and past the fresh-faced parkour kids by the Hayward Gallery, then rebelling fiercely against its own sweet image much as the leaping teens are, jinking violently toward the barrier and counterpointing its endearing greenness with a maelstrom of jarring orange sparks. The fountains of shattered glass look almost like fireworks, a neat callback to a dozen New Year sound-and-light shows enjoyed from this very spot, cascading myriad colours across the tarmac and illuminating the grey with paroxysms of kaleidoscopic vividity. The barrier folds with what feels like inevitability, catching and crushing pedestrians in its jagged crook as it creases like paper, the car bumping onto the pavement and mowing down tourist after startled tourist, commuter after astounded commuter, a trail of souls whispering upward in its wake, joining us in the atmosphere and spreading out across London, each one searching for home, or a significant other, or an answer, or simply somewhere else to be.

"The barrier was a good place to hide," Mum says, tightening her grip on my hand almost imperceptibly, but just enough to tell me that she knows, she knows, and it's alright, really, everything's fine, let the anxiety just bleed away. "It's a shame it didn't work, but how were you to know?"

"Perhaps I did know."

"Well, that's neither here nor there at this stage, darling."

"I suppose not."

The birds, hundreds of them, perhaps thousands, maintaining a respectful distance and lining up along the railings of Blackfriars, a mighty chorus to the ragdoll marionettes scattered across Waterloo Bridge.

"And will he be joining us?"

"No, your father still has plenty to do. See, he has all of those other people to take care of."

And there's Wilson, calmly stepping between the bodies as the whirlwind of paramedics scurry around the rouge-drenched scene, scribbling notes on his pad with that fancy marbled Parker, talking into the radio on his lapel, cataloguing the chaos and shuffling everything into order, and then he's beside me, and he stops, and double-takes at my crumpled and devastated body, and he collapses to the ground, adrift in the huge crimson halo that surrounds me, holding me tight and howling, and he turns and looks up, straight up towards us, and then his head is in his hands.

"You're not angry, mummy?"

"No. Not angry at all."

"And we can leave now?"

"Yes, son. It's fine. We can leave."

Printed in Great
Britain
by Amazon

31953442R00092